"We will not accept charity."

"I need a good cook, and it would give you a roof over your head. Please? You'll be doing me a great favor." Will waited until Emmeline finally nodded.

"All right. Hopefully, it will just be for a few days. I don't know how to thank you, Mr. Logan."

"You can begin by calling me Will," he suggested.

"If I am to be in your employ, I should not be so familiar."

Will could tell she had slipped into a subservient position and he didn't like that. In a way Emmeline was behaving wisely. If she remained in High Plains, keeping her good name would be crucial to finding a husband and making a new life for herself.

That thought hit Will like a punch in the stomach. Most young women chose to marry and raise families.

It was the idea of Emmeline Carter as a bride that stuck in his craw.

After the Storm: The Founding Years
A tornado can't tear apart the fabric of faith
and love in a frontier Kansas town.

Books by Valerie Hansen

Love Inspired Historical

Frontier Courtship
Wilderness Courtship
High Plains Bride

Love Inspired Suspense

*Her Brother's Keeper
The Danger Within
*Out of the Depths
Deadly Payoff
Shadow of Turning
Hidden in the Wall
*Nowhere to Run
No Alibi

*Serenity, Arkansas

Love Inspired

*The Wedding Arbor
*The Troublesome Angel
*The Perfect Couple
*Second Chances
*Love One Another
*Blessings of the Heart
*Samantha's Gift
*Everlasting Love
The Hamilton Heir
*A Treasure of the Heart
Healing the Boss's Heart*

VALERIE HANSEN

was thirty when she awoke to the presence of the Lord in her life and turned to Jesus. In the years that followed she worked with young children, both in church and secular environments. She also raised a family of her own and played foster mother to a wide assortment of furred and feathered critters.

Married to her high school sweetheart since age seventeen, she now lives in an old farmhouse she and her husband renovated with their own hands. She loves to hike the wooded hills behind the house and reflect on the marvelous turn her life has taken. Not only is she privileged to reside among the loving, accepting folks in the breathtakingly beautiful Ozark Mountains of Arkansas, she also gets to share her personal faith by telling the stories of her heart for all of Steeple Hill's Love Inspired lines.

Life doesn't get much better than that!

Many are the plans in a man's heart,
but it is the Lord's purpose that prevails.
—*Proverbs* 19:21

Special thanks to the two other authors who participated with me in the series
After the Storm: The Founding Years,
Renee Ryan and Victoria Bylin

Getting to know both these talented writers as we've worked and plotted together has been a real blessing.

Prologue

Kansas Territory
1858

The two solitary riders felt the brunt of the wintry wind at their backs as they urged their weary mounts toward the closest high point in the flint hills. Both men were wrapped in buffalo robes they'd obtained from the Plains Indians they'd encountered near the abandoned Kansa Mission School at Council Grove.

Will Logan, in the lead, was glad they'd brought enough baubles with them to successfully trade for the thick, hairy robes. Though the hides weren't the sweetest-smelling things he'd ever encountered, without their protection he and his friend would literally be freezing.

He pulled his broad-brimmed, felt hat lower and

bent forward in the saddle, bracing against the force of the prairie gale and wishing mightily that he'd had the foresight to grow a beard and let his thick, dark blond hair reach his shoulders instead of keeping it so neatly trimmed.

His fingers were half-numb inside his leather gloves as he tugged on the rope fastened to their pack mule's harness, urging the stubborn animal to keep pace. Although it plodded along in begrudging compliance, the rangy mule laid its ears back, snorted and blew clouds of condensation from its nostrils, clearly not agreeing that the small party was behaving sensibly by leaving the known route and pressing on into uncharted territory.

"Just a few hundred yards more," Will shouted to his human companion.

Zeb Garrison kicked his bay gelding and pulled up beside Will's sorrel. "So you say. I should have known better than to follow you out here in December. We're both likely to freeze to death. And the horses, too."

Will laughed in spite of the icy needles of frost pricking his cheeks and nose. "You got soft working in Boston," he taunted. "This change will be good for both of us. You'll see. And by getting an early start, we're far enough ahead of other settlers to lay claim to the choicest plots of land in this neck of the woods."

"Assuming we live long enough to enjoy them," Zeb countered. "If the weather doesn't kill us, those

Indians we keep seeing in the distance might. I still say they're tracking us. Probably want their buffalo hides back."

"Nonsense. We bought them fair and square."

With one final lunge, the horses gained the high ground. Will's pale blue eyes widened, and he shaded them with his hand on his brow, sighing deeply. Below lay total vindication, as lush a valley as he'd ever hoped for and the wide, meandering river that completed their list of necessities. Too bad his doubting father was not here to see what he'd found.

Rising in his stirrups, Will turned to his lifelong friend, pointed and grinned. "There. See? I told you we'd find the perfect place for your mill and my ranch. I can picture it already. The town will go down there, thanks to the generosity of the New England Emigrant Aid Company, and I can use my stake from them to bring in longhorns to graze these hills. Eating switchgrass and big and little bluestem the likes of what grows here in summer will fatten up those critters real fast. They'll be ready for market in two shakes of a lamb's tail."

Zeb's nod was barely perceptible beneath the bulky buffalo robe, but he did agree. "Maybe you're right. It does look promising. I think I even see a small waterfall upstream that I can use for power. Still…"

Will wasn't about to take no for an answer. He'd prayed continually for the good Lord's guidance and knew without question that this was his personal promised land.

He passed the mule's lead rope to Zeb, then gave his horse its head and let the animal choose the best route of descent from the wide mesa to the river valley below. Will was so exuberant he paid no heed as the animal's shod hooves loosened bits of shale and ice that skittered down ahead of them like a miniature avalanche. This was his Eden. He knew it with all his heart and soul.

He had already dismounted on a flat rise of land near the frigid but swiftly flowing river when his friend reined in and joined him.

"Here!" Will shouted excitedly. He spread his arms wide as he spoke, ignoring the buffalo robe slipping off the shoulders of his coat and falling onto the shallow accumulation of snow. "The main street will go across here, abreast of the river, and your mill can be upstream so you can either freight the lumber to town or float it if the water's high enough. It's perfect." His grin widened. "Come on. Admit it. I was right."

Zeb dismounted, ground-hitched his horse and tied off the mule's lead rope to a sturdy cottonwood tree. "All right. I'll go along this time. Just remember, this whole trip was my idea to begin with."

Laughing, Will shook his head. "Sure, boss me around the way you did when we were boys. You may have money of your own but I had the brains and foresight to convince others to finance me." He ducked as Zeb feinted a punch to his shoulder. "Grab the hammer and some stakes. We're home. We'll call it High Plains."

He sobered as they paced off the land and then drove the final stake to mark their claim. Removing his hat despite the icy wind that ruffled his hair, he dropped to his knees atop the thick buffalo hide and bowed his head. Zeb did the same.

"Lord, we thank You for bringing us to this place and we dedicate this portion of High Plains, Kansas Territory, to You," Will prayed aloud. "Keep us mindful of Your plan and continue to guide our paths."

Zeb echoed his "Amen" and the two young pioneers rose. "Merry Christmas," he told Will, frowning. "I sure hope you're right about this being the right place."

"It is," his smiling friend assured him. "And a very Merry Christmas to you, too."

Chapter One

The farther west their wagon train proceeded, the more Emmeline Carter missed her former home in central Missouri. The political climate back there had been in constant upheaval, especially since the hanging of the abolitionist John Brown in Virginia a scant six months before. Still, it was the only home she'd ever known, and life on the trail had her missing that sense of security.

Although there had been recent fighting amongst her former neighbors to the point of bloodshed, what was to say that life would be any better in Oregon? The fact that her taciturn father insisted so was not nearly enough to convince Emmeline.

So far, the journey by covered wagon had been

trying but not altogether unpleasant. Word among the other women was that there would be many terrible trials to come during their months-long pilgrimage, but Emmeline was willing to wait and see rather than borrow trouble.

One of the worst naysayers had told Emmeline, just that morning, "You'll soon see, my girl. There'll be many a fresh grave along the trail before we reach our new homes. If cholera don't get us, those horrid Indians will. I shudder to think what they'll do to you and your pretty sisters, especially."

"Then I shall pray earnestly that we don't encounter hostiles," Emmeline had replied, continuing to prepare the morning meal for her family while her sickly mother remained abed in the wagon, and her father, Amos, and brother, Johnny, tended to the oxen.

"Bess, Glory, fetch the twins," she called, using that as an opportunity to cease listening to the dire predictions of the older woman whose wagon was parked next to theirs. "The biscuits are almost done."

Emmeline knew that such rumors of catastrophe had to have some basis in fact. It had been frightening to leave home and hearth and start a journey into unfamiliar territory, especially since their already ample family of six now encompassed orphans Missy and Mikey, as well. Yet she was encouraged by the way everyone had helped gather firewood and dried buffalo chips for the fires and had taken turns caring for Mama when she was ill. Even little Glory had taken a turn. So had the eight-year-old twins.

If Mama had had her way she would have adopted their neighbors' children outright after their parents both sickened and died so suddenly. It was only by divine providence that Papa had allowed her to bring them along in the hopes of eventually finding them a permanent home. Thankfully, they were small for their age and didn't eat much. Keeping stocked with proper provisions to tide them over between supply stops was always a worry.

The responsibility of doing so had, of course, fallen to Emmeline, which was why she had walked from their camp to town after breakfast and was now getting ready to enter the prairie mercantile. This little town seemed peaceful enough, she mused. Perhaps the territories would be safer, less politically volatile, than her home state had been. As long as her father was around, however, a certain amount of trouble would keep dogging their path no matter where they went.

Emmeline felt like a mother hen as she shooed her brother and sisters and the orphan twins up the wooden steps and into the small store in her father's wake. Since her mother, Joanna, had stayed in her bed in the covered wagon and sworn she could not manage to rise, Emmeline had had to once again assume charge of the children.

Fifteen-year-old Bess, four years her junior, was helpful in this kind of situation, of course, but Johnny, the next youngest, was worse than useless. She'd thought he was as bad as he could get at twelve. When he'd recently turned thirteen, however, she'd realized that his rowdy years were just beginning.

Since she'd had the foresight to braid her hair and fasten it at her nape, she pushed her slat bonnet back and let it hang by its ribbons to help cool her head and neck. The morning was already sultry to the point of being burdensome in more ways than one. It intensified the strong odors of leather and spices and salted meats inside the store till they nearly made her ill. Rivulets of perspiration pasted tiny wisps of loose hair to her temples.

And it's only June, she thought, trying to keep her spirits up by sheer force of will.

"Bess, dear, you watch after the twins," Emmeline ordered kindly. "Johnny, keep your hands to yourself. You know the rules. No penny candy."

She hoisted five-year-old Glory, the youngest, on her hip and removed the child's bonnet too. Together they wended their way past kegs of molasses, sacks of flour and other sundry supplies that were piled on the rough plank floor and stacked high on shelves that lined the walls all the way to the low ceiling. Various kitchen utensils and farm tools were suspended from the rough-hewn rafters, making the store seem even more overcrowded.

A man who was clad as a cowboy, dusty from his labors, turned to glance at her as she approached the counter to place the family's order. Her father had already joined a group of men who were loudly discussing the conditions of the trail ahead of them and Emmeline knew that the mundane tasks had, as usual, been left to her.

The cowboy at the counter had already removed his broad-brimmed hat to show slicked-back, dark blond hair that curled slightly. His blue eyes seemed to twinkle as he nodded politely and wished her a "Good morning, ma'am," without being formally introduced first.

Emmeline knew social mores were more relaxed on the trail, but her strict upbringing nevertheless caused her to hesitate before she replied with a terse "Good morning." Seconds later, when he continued to speak, she realized that the man was assuming she was the mother of all these children! What an appalling notion.

"You have a lovely family," he said, ruffling Johnny's hair to distract him just as the boy was surreptitiously slipping his hand into a candy jar.

Emmeline, gritting her teeth, said merely, "Thank you," and gave her brother a scathing look. Then she turned her attention to the pinch-faced, portly woman behind the counter. "How do you do. We haven't been on the trail long, so we don't require much, but I was told it was best to keep my larders stocked."

"That, it is," the proprietress said as if addressing a nitwit. She accepted the list Emmeline was holding, then leaned closer to speak more quietly. "You're mighty young to have so many children. How did you manage it?" She briefly eyed Emmeline's father. "Marry a man with a passel of 'em already?"

"No. That's my father, Amos Carter, and these are my brother and sisters," Emmeline explained, taking care to raise her voice enough to disabuse the cowboy of her supposed motherhood. "Except for the twins over there. We're taking them to Oregon with us in the hopes of finding them good homes."

"I might be interested myself if they was old enough or strong enough to be of use round the store," the woman said. "How old are they?"

"Eight, but they've had a hard life so they're small for their age."

"I'll say. Plum useless, if you ask me."

Hoping that Missy and Mikey had not overheard the woman's cutting remarks, Emmeline noted that Bess was teaching them to play checkers at a small table next to the unlit, barrel-shaped, wood stove. Happily, their attention to the checkerboard and the overall din of conversation within the small store had apparently rendered them oblivious to the woman's unkindness.

The cowboy, however, was far from unaware. "Excuse me for saying so, Mrs. Johnson," he drawled, barely smiling at the older woman, "but don't you think it would be wiser to keep such untoward opinions to yourself?"

The proprietress huffed, "Well, I never," and turned to go about her business, leaving Emmeline and the friendly stranger standing at the counter together.

"Thank you," she said, meaning it sincerely. "The twins have had a difficult year since they lost their parents. They're just now beginning to act like normal children again."

"My pleasure, miss." He bowed slightly. "The name's Will Logan. I own a little spread south and west of here. The Circle-L. Maybe you've heard of it?"

"I'm sorry, no. I'm merely a traveler passing through. But I'm sure your ranch is lovely."

He chuckled. "Well...I wouldn't say that, exactly. Not yet, anyway. Give it time. I've only been in these parts for a little while, myself." Gesturing at the store building, he added, "My friend and I founded High Plains just a year and a half ago. It's his mill that's been providing most of the lumber for the town, of late."

"Even that magnificent church house we passed just east of here?"

"You can thank our town ladies and the New England Emigrant Aid Company for that," Will admitted. "The door and windows were shipped from Boston and so was some of the finer wood for the interior. But the structure itself took shape right here in High Plains."

"Then you should be very proud, Mr. Logan."

Will grinned and shook his head. "I try hard not to be too highfalutin. Don't want the good Lord to get mad 'cause I took the credit for His work."

"I'm sure that building the big church will satisfy Him," Emmeline said, noting that her companion did not appear to agree. His smile faded and he seemed to be studying her.

Finally, he said, "I doubt that the Father, the creator of 'many mansions' is too impressed by any building man makes." He replaced his hat and touched the brim politely. "Well, if you all will excuse me, I have to stop at the mill and then head back to my spread. I wish you and yours Godspeed, miss."

Watching the broad-shouldered, appealing rancher turn and start toward the door, Emmeline was taken by how optimistic he had seemed in spite of the obvious hardships inherent in his line of work, not to mention starting from scratch and building an entire town in the space of just a few years. What an admirable man. His attitude served to make him quite attractive indeed.

She supposed she would need that kind of extraordinary fortitude—and more—to face the rest of her journey. She just hoped she was up to it. Taking charge of her siblings and the twins wasn't new to her. It was being in unfamiliar territory that gave her pause. Still, as long as they were together, as a family, she supposed they'd manage to cope.

The idea of family caused her to glance over at her father and shiver in spite of the humidity and high temperature inside the stuffy mercantile. Papa might not be the meanest man in the world, but he had to be close to the top of the list.

Emmeline had spent most of her life trying to placate him and protect both her mother and her siblings from his unpredictable fits of temper. That was why she'd never marry or otherwise leave home. Papa had wasted his breath ordering her to stay until little Glory was raised. She wouldn't have abandoned her sisters, her ill mother or even troublesome Johnny. Not under any circumstances.

The Garrison mill sat west of High Plains proper, a little past Zeb's impressive, whitewashed, two-story house. Will found his old friend working on the cutting floor instead of sitting behind the desk in his small office.

"Morning," Will called, having to shout to be heard over the sound of sawing.

Zeb grinned, waved a greeting and loped toward him. "What brings you to town?"

"Just needed a few things over at Johnson's. And I want to order some two-by-six planks from you. I'm finally going to put a floor in the bunkhouse. There's no hurry, though. I've got all summer to finish the job."

"Good, because we're running near capacity."

"Even now? I thought the rush was over."

Zeb wiped his brow with a handkerchief as he gestured downriver. "Nope. Guess some of those new settlers are tired of living in tents and wagons. They're planning to build real houses and maybe a business or two. Good for them, I say—good for all of us."

"Yeah, definitely. It'll be nice to see the town continue to grow. I'm amazed it's come this far in such a short time."

"Hey," Zeb drawled with a lazy grin, "you told me this was the perfect place to build. I'm just glad to see that so many others agree with you."

"So am I. Start my order out with forty boards, as long as twelve feet if you've got 'em. Once I've used those I'll see what else I need."

"Done. Where you headed now?"

"Home. I've got plenty to do. Those heifers are dropping more calves every day. See you Sunday?"

"Of course. Can't miss church or Cassandra would have my hide." He chuckled. "I think my sister wants an escort more than anything else so she can show off those new dresses and hats of hers. What better place than in church?"

"And it also might do your soul some good," Will gibed.

"You just mind your own soul and I'll look after mine," Zeb shot back. He eyed the sky. "Take care riding home. The weather looks a bit changeable."

"Will do. And you try to keep the sawdust out of your boots."

"That'll be the day."

Will was still laughing at their parting exchange when he mounted up, gave his horse its head and let it start home without much guidance.

It was just as well that the sorrel was used to the trail, he mused, because he was preoccupied by thoughts of the pretty young woman he'd just met in Johnson's mercantile. She couldn't have been more than nineteen or twenty years of age, yet she'd had the sober bearing of a much older person, as if she were carrying the weight of the world on those slim shoulders.

"And little wonder," he muttered, recalling the way she'd had to keep the children in line and handle the shopping while her father wasted time talking with other men. Will frowned as he thought of the derogatory references he'd overheard her father make about her as he'd passed the raucous group of men on his way out of the store. The old man was obviously cruel and vindictive. If he also drank to excess, as Will's own father had, that poor young woman was trapped in an unspeakable home situation. And so were her siblings.

Racking his brain, Will tried to recall the girl's name and failed to come up with anything except that her father was Amos Carter, her brother was Johnny and the orphans had similar names that each started with an *M*. She must not have mentioned her own name, he concluded, because he surely would have remembered. Everything else about her, from the deep blue eyes that matched the color of her dress to her dark, silky hair was crystal clear.

And speaking of dark things, he added, growing concerned as he glanced at the sky, it was starting to look as if Zeb's weather prediction was right. The previously empty sky was beginning to cloud up and show signs of an impending storm. Will could see for miles once he topped the hills to the southwest and it was obvious that the weather was about to change for the worse.

Pausing, he looked back at the beautiful, placid river valley and the fledgling town he'd helped found. The church spire to the east and Zeb's mill to the west framed a Main Street lined with half a dozen stores. Across Main, backed up against the river and parked beneath a grove of cottonwoods, sat the ragtag group of temporary tents, shacks and wagons that Zeb had mentioned.

Those shelters would offer little protection against the upcoming storm. Will could only hope that the settlers would find refuge somewhere safe. The frequently occurring severe storms on the open plains could be dangerous—even deadly. And it looked as if they were in for another deluge within the next few hours.

Spurring his horse, he headed for his ranch at a

brisk canter. There wasn't a lot he could do for the longhorns he had grazing on the open prairie on both sides of the river, but it was sensible to send a few hands, including himself, to try to prevent a stampede among the critters closest to his house and barn. He just hoped a herd of nervous buffalo didn't decide to run over his corn plot or trample his corrals the way one had during a bad lightning storm last summer. This storm was coming in fast, and would probably hit hard, pushing the livestock into a frenzy.

He pressed onward, hoping and praying that his instincts were wrong, yet positive that they were not.

The wind had increased and the sky had darkened menacingly by the time he reined in between the main ranch house and the barn. Several of his hands were already mounted and had bridled an extra horse, apparently awaiting his return, while the rangy ranch dogs barked excitedly and circled the riders.

"Clint, you and Bob take the south ridge," Will shouted. "I'll ride more west, then circle back to you." He gestured as he dismounted. "This looks like a bad one."

"Yeah, boss," the lanky cowhand replied. "It ain't gonna be pretty, that's a fact. You want a fresh mount?"

"Yes." Will threw a stirrup over his saddle horn and began to loosen his cinch. "Where's Hank?"

"Already forded the river to try to round up the stragglers over there."

"Good man."

Clint nodded and passed the reins of the extra horse to Will, then spurred his mount and headed south with his partner as instructed.

Left alone, Will switched his saddle to the fresh horse, turned his tired sorrel into a corral and mounted up. He'd thought about taking the time to close the storm shutters on the house but had decided he shouldn't delay getting to the herd. A building could be replaced fairly easily and besides, Hank was no longer inside where he could be hurt if it collapsed. Should this weather spawn a tornado, as Will feared it might, the old ranch cook would be much safer riding the range with him and the others, anyway.

Spurring the new horse, he raced toward open country. "Thank the good Lord I don't have a wife and family to look after, too," he muttered prayerfully.

His mind immediately jumped to the settlers in town, and the ones in the wagon train—to the pretty young woman in charge of so many children. Surely her father, or whoever was leading their party, would be wise enough to tarry in High Plains until the weather improved.

Emmeline was walking beside the family's slowly moving, ox-pulled wagon while her mother lay inside on a narrow tick filled with straw and covered by a quilt.

Ruts in the trail made the wagon's wooden wheels and axles bind and squeal as they bounced in and out of the depressions and jarred everyone and everything. Pots rattled. Chickens hanging in handmade crates along the outside of the wagon panted, squawked and jockeyed for space and footing on the slatted floors of their wooden boxes. The team plodded along, slow but sure, barely working to move the heavy wagon on the fairly level terrain.

Glory had quickly tired of walking. Emmeline had carried her on one hip for a while, then put her inside with their mother, in spite of the ailing woman's protests that she simply could not cope with even one of her offspring.

Hoping that her father couldn't hear her softly speaking, Emmeline gripped the top of the rear tailboard to steady herself and whispered hoarsely, "Hush." She raised her head and gestured toward the man walking beside the oxen and prodding them with a staff when they faltered. "You know you'll make Papa mad again if you raise a fuss."

She hated having to be so cautious all the time, but the alternative was a beating for anyone within the wiry, older man's reach, and she felt bound to try to protect the others. She'd had to do that more and more frequently, of late.

The sky was so dark at the horizon it seemed almost black, with a ribbon of pale sky showing beneath, as if a table sat atop a thin strip of the heavens visible only nearest the ground. Emmeline had seen weather like this back in Missouri, although not often. If she had been at home she would have gathered her siblings and shooed them into the root cellar for safety. Here on the plains she had no such option, much to her chagrin.

She hiked her skirts slightly to facilitate faster movement. A dozen swift steps brought her even with Amos and she easily kept pace. "Papa?"

"What do you want, girl?"

"Look at that sky. I'm worried."

"I seen it. Don't you go tellin' me how to think, you hear? I been in storms worse'n this before and I'm still kickin'."

"Yes, but—"

"Hush. Just because you're nearly growed that don't make you smarter'n me. I've been takin' care of this family for longer than you've been on this earth and we're all still here." He glowered at her. "Well? You gonna waste the whole day naggin' me or are you gonna go look after your mama?"

"Mama's fine," Emmeline insisted bravely, although she did put more distance between herself and the reach of her father's heavy wooden staff. "She and Glory are taking a nap."

Amos cursed under his breath. "Useless woman. I should've got me a younger wife long ago."

It wasn't the first time Emmeline had heard him

say such mean-spirited things. She couldn't imagine what her poor mama felt like when Papa talked like that. Little wonder Mama stayed in a sickbed so much. If and when she did arise, she had to face her husband and take more of his verbal—and physical—abuse.

Shading her eyes beneath the brim of her bonnet and squinting into the distance, Emmeline tensed. She hadn't thought those clouds could possibly look any worse but they did. Rain was falling in the far distance, evidenced by slanted sheets of gray that streamed from the solid cloud layer toward the prairie in visible waves, indicating a downpour ahead.

She spun to scan the surrounding terrain. Darkness at midday was everywhere. Encroaching. Threatening. And the wind from the southwest was increasing, heralding the kind of destructive, unpredictable storm that she'd dreaded.

Emmeline shivered and pulled her shawl more tightly around her shoulders. If all they got from this weather was soaked to the skin and muddy, she'd count it a boon. In similar storms that she'd experienced back home, such signs of impending peril were not taken lightly.

She squinted. The kinds of menacing clouds she was looking at right now were capable of dealing a blow that could mean serious injury, loss of property—and perhaps even death.

Chapter Two

Now that Will was riding the high ground and could see for literally miles, his concern for High Plains increased. If he'd been a gambling man, which he was not, he'd have given even odds that his friends and their families would soon be in mortal danger.

Wind from the west and south was increasing, driving bits of stinging dirt and broken vegetation against his clothing and exposed hands and face. He crammed his hat on tighter, turned his back to the onslaught and fought to quiet his horse while he unrolled the slicker that had been tied behind the cantle of his saddle. The animal was clearly agitated, and well it should be under these circumstances, Will reasoned.

"Easy boy. Easy. We'll be fine."

As soon as he'd donned the slicker, he leaned low

in the saddle and patted the horse's lathered neck to try to reassure it, wishing he believed his own placating words.

Looking south, he saw that Clint and Bob had rounded up a large portion of his herd and were driving them in a tight circle to keep them controlled. Off to his right by about twenty degrees, an immense dust cloud was rising to meet the gray, somber heavens. The wind carried the sounds of shrill bleating and the rumbling drum of hundreds of cloven hooves.

So that's what has my horse so riled up. Will put voice to his conclusion and patted the nervous animal again. "Buffalo. No wonder you're so jumpy, boy. I am, too, now that I can tell what you smelled."

Reining hard, he kicked the horse into a gallop and raced to join his men. This was just the beginning of what promised to be one of the wildest days he'd experienced since settling in the flint hills. He just hoped he and his men survived whatever test the weather had in store.

Amos had finally halted the Carters' covered wagon, much to Emmeline's relief. By that point, she had to shout at him to be heard over the howling wind. If she had not been wearing her bonnet she knew her cheeks would have already been blasted raw by the wind-driven prairie dirt and bits of broken vegetation that stung in spite of her clothing.

"What about the other wagons?" she screeched. "They stopped a half hour ago. Are we going to turn back and join them?"

"No need," her father insisted. "We'll just wait here a bit till the dust settles."

She couldn't believe his stubbornness. Not now. Not when they were in the middle of nowhere and basically alone. If it had been up to her she'd have at least tried to find a rock outcropping or gulley in which to shelter. Anything had to be better than just standing out in the open and taking so much punishment.

Hurrying to the rear of the wagon, she called to her sister Bess, who had taken up a position on the leeward side and was holding Missy's and Mikey's hands. "Take the twins off the trail and try to find some safe place to hunker down. I'll bring Mama and Glory," Emmeline shouted.

"What about Johnny?" Bess replied.

"Papa needs him to help calm the team." *Besides,* she added to herself, instantly penitent, *Johnny's like Papa, too mean to get hurt.*

She knew such thoughts had to be a sin, but she couldn't help herself. If there was ever a mirror image of her father, it was her thirteen-year-old brother. Thank the Lord Bess and Glory were girls!

Emmeline watched as Bess tugged the fair-haired twins off the wide, rutted trail and into the thick stands of big and little bluestem. Surely there would be some hidey-hole out there. There had to be. Even the shallow depression of a buffalo wallow would be better than remaining in the wagon, which was already being rocked sideways by the strong winds.

She leaned her head and shoulders in over the tailboard and shouted, "Come with me, Mama. You and Glory will be safer outside."

Joanna vehemently resisted as she clung to the five-year-old. "No. We're staying right here. Your papa will take care of us."

"Against *this?*"

Emmeline knew she was screeching at her poor mother, but she felt such tactics were necessary, given the dire circumstances. With the wind catching the fabric of her dress and petticoats and whipping them like an unfettered sail, she could barely stay on her feet. Soon, it would be impossible for any of them to successfully flee. If it wasn't already too late.

"Yes," Joanna said. "I'm not moving from this wagon and neither is my baby. If you want to run off and desert us, then go. I'm not holding you here."

"Yes, you are," Emmeline told her. "I won't leave you."

"And I won't leave your father."

"After the way he's always treated you? How can you say that?"

"He's my husband. I took holy vows and I intend to honor them," Joanna said flatly. "Come in here with us, all of you."

Glancing at the tall prairie grasses that were now slashing around like buggy whips and bending nearly flat to the ground Emmeline prayed that Bess and the twins had found suitable shelter. It was too late to go after them now. She'd have no chance of finding them in this turmoil.

She swiveled slowly, guarding her face by pressing the sides of her slat bonnet closer to her cheeks. Rain was beginning to fall in drops the size of apricot pits. That meant the whirling dust would no longer be so vexing, but that was little comfort, since hail was now starting to pelt her, too. It stung her skin like an assault of vicious hornets, striking her head, hands, arms and shoulders until she had to bite her lip to keep from crying out in pain.

That was enough to spur immediate action. Emmeline grabbed the tailgate of the wagon and leaped, hoisting herself over it and tumbling head-first into the straw-filled ticking beside her mother and youngest sister.

They reached out and embraced each other tightly, though their respite from nature's onslaught was brief. Larger chunks of hail soon began to puncture the canvas roof, each impact making the rends in the fabric bigger, wider.

Wind then grabbed the loosening sheets, lifted and tore them, increasing the damage until there was little covering the wagon's occupants except a few shreds of canvas, the bare bows and the bedding they clung to for what little protection it offered.

"Hang on!" Emmeline screamed, grabbing Glory more tightly and holding her close to shield the child with her own body.

Joanna was screeching, "Amos!" over and over again, to no avail.

Even if he had been close at hand, Emmeline knew he could not have heard anyone's cries over the increasing roar of the storm.

It built until it was so deafening it made her ears ache and pop as if she were descending a mountain trail at a gallop. Suction from the spinning torrent pulled at her, foretelling what was about to happen.

"Twister!" Emmeline screamed at the top of her lungs.

She threw herself and Glory over their mother and clung to them both for dear life. Her calico skirt was tearing. Her bonnet was snatched from her head in spite of its tightly tied ribbons and her hair fanned out in a wild tangle, stinging her skin as it slapped her cheeks and neck.

Suddenly, she sensed herself being lifted until she felt weightless. She spun. Tumbled. Cracked the top of her head on one of the bows that arched over the wagon.

The rest of the world passed before her eyes in a fierce blur of colors accompanied by a painful, incessant battering and a dizzying disorientation beyond any she had ever experienced.

Still grasping Glory and trying to protect her small, fragile body with her own, Emmeline was carried away from their mother, from the battered wagon and its heavy-bodied ox team.

Praying wordlessly, thoughtlessly, she imagined that she'd glimpsed the team and wagon in the distance before she'd squeezed her eyes shut to try and stop her vertigo.

That sight had been so fleeting, so tenuous, she wasn't positive it wasn't imaginary. All she knew for certain was that they had been overtaken by an enormous twister and were totally at its mercy.

Please, God, let the others be all right.

That was the last lucid thought Emmeline had before blackness overcame her.

Will managed to reach his men and the milling cattle herd before the buffalo crested the nearest rise.

"You think you can handle 'em?" he shouted to Clint.

"Yeah." The other man pointed. "Can you turn that mess before it gets to us?"

"I'll try."

Hoping to divert the hundreds of stampeding wild buffalo, Will shouted and repeatedly fired his pistol in the air while spurring his reluctant horse to charge straight at them.

The lead bulls faltered little. On they ran, their sharp hooves churning the prairie and raising clouds of acrid dust that was caught by the fierce wind and driven against man and beast to sting like a myriad of tiny needles.

Fear pricked Will, too. He'd heard that bison were as easily redirected as cattle. He sure hoped that was true because unless they turned soon, there wouldn't be enough left of him to find, let alone bury in the churchyard.

"Yah, yah," he shouted, continuing to point his pistol in the air and fire. If he'd had his rifle loaded and ready he'd have tried to drop the leaders. Since he didn't have that option at the moment he'd just have to persevere. And pray fervently that his method was successful.

About the time Will was getting ready to wheel his horse and try to make a dash to safety, the bulls running in front of the herd began to lead the others in a wide arc, avoiding the longhorn herd—and its owner—by a goodly margin.

Satisfied, Will reined in and raised in his stirrups to survey the distant plains while heavy rain continued to fall. He couldn't see much to the west through the sheeting water, but it had to be plenty bad over that way. It didn't look much better in the direction of his ranch house, either.

Well, that couldn't be helped. The steers were the most important thing he owned. They were his livelihood. Everything else could fairly easily be replaced if it was damaged. He just hoped they hadn't had too many newborn spring calves trampled beneath the hooves of the frightened, milling cattle or knocked unconscious by the hail, and that the men chasing down stragglers hadn't been harmed.

Shading his eyes and peering into the distance, he tried to make out any signs of the wagon train that he'd encountered in High Plains. They'd still been encamped when he'd left town. Hopefully, they weren't caught in the maelstrom he could see from the hilltop. If they were, God help them.

Relative calm soon followed the twister. Emmeline awoke to feel rain bathing her hair, her face and what was left of her favorite calico frock. She sat up slowly and wiped her muddy hands on her skirt before pushing her long hair back. It was not only loose and hopelessly tangled, it was matted with bits of straw, mud and goodness-knows-what-else that had come from the prairie.

The cool rain helped bring her to her senses and she raised her face to the heavens to wash her cheeks and help clear the irritating motes from her eyes.

Blinking, she drew a deep, shaky breath. Her ribs hurt a tad when she did so, but she didn't think they were broken. At least not badly. And although her head was pounding and she had to continually try to clear her vision, the rest of her seemed to be in pretty fair shape, except for a few small cuts and scrapes. But what about the others?

Her heart leaped, her senses fully returning. "Glory!"

Quickly scanning her surroundings, Emmeline tried to spot her baby sister. Her hopes were dashed when she failed. She staggered to her feet, bracing against the milder wind that remained, and cupped her hands around her mouth. "Glory, answer me. Where are you?"

Soft weeping was the only reply.

Following that sound she soon found the little girl seated on the ground, grasping her bent knees and rocking back and forth.

Emmeline knelt and took the child in her arms. "Praise the Lord! Are you all right, Glory, honey?"

"I want Mama."

Mama. Emmeline's heart sped like the horrid wind that had decimated their party as her thoughts finally caught up to harsh reality. *Where was Mama?*

She was glad the rain falling on her face masked her tears because when she turned and spotted the remains of all their worldly possessions she couldn't help weeping openly. Their heavy wagon lay on its top, wheels in the air like the feet of a long-dead prairie dog, and there was no sign of Papa and Johnny.

Where Mama had ended up was another question.

If she was still in the inverted wagon, there was no possible way Emmeline could free her. Not without help.

And, thanks to Papa's stubbornness, there was no way to tell how long it would be before anyone else knew what had befallen them. No way at all.

"Dear Jesus, help us. Help us all," she prayed in a whisper as she lifted her little sister and started to carry her toward the wreckage.

Glory clung to her neck and sobbed. Emmeline was so concerned about their mother's fate she was nearly back to the wagon before it occurred to her that Bess and the twins were unaccounted for, too!

Saying another quick prayer for her sister and the eight-year-olds, Emmeline approached the upset wagon cautiously. She was afraid of letting Glory see death for the first time in her short life.

As a small child, Emmeline had watched her maternal grandmother's passing and had never gotten that image out of her mind, even though it had been a peaceful scene. Seeing their dear mother injured, or worse, would be terribly hard for a five-year-old to bear.

Emmeline called, "Mama," and was rewarded by an answering call. It was muffled, due to the positioning of the upturned wagon, but strong nevertheless. Her tears became those of relief and joy.

"Mama? Are you stuck under there?"

"Yes. Go get your papa to help you get me out."

"Okay. I'll leave Glory here to talk to you."

Joanna's voice broke. "My baby's all right? You both are? I thought…I was afraid…"

"We're fine, Mama. Wet and muddy but otherwise fine." She placed the little girl next to the wagon and told her to stay there, realizing that that command probably wouldn't have been necessary. The child was already fully engrossed in chattering to their mother and wiggling her tiny fingers through narrow cracks in the wagon bed while she related their harrowing adventure. The scene was so touching it brought fresh tears to Emmeline's eyes.

Cautiously circling the broken wreckage and trying to avoid the small patches of piled-up hail that the rain had not yet melted, Emmeline came upon one of their faithful oxen lying dead in its traces. Apparently, when the wagon had flipped over, the abrupt motion had snapped that poor animal's neck and it had fallen where it stood.

The other side of the double yoke had broken, freeing the surviving ox, Big Jack. He stood apart from the carnage, trembling and staring at the death scene but apparently unhurt.

Johnny stood beside the lumbering animal, hugging its muscular neck and weeping like the child he still was.

Knowing there was nothing to be done for the dead animal, Emmeline went to her brother and gently touched his shoulder. "Are you okay?"

He nodded rapidly, hiding his face from his sister by pressing it to Big Jack's slick, brown hide.

"Where's Papa?" She held her breath and waited for his answer, never dreaming he'd turn and point back at the wagon tongue.

With that, the boy began to wail in earnest.

Emmeline spun around, her heart pounding, her breath catching in her throat. He couldn't mean… Her eyes widened with shock. Clearly, he did.

She'd been so upset over the death of the faithful ox, she'd failed to look beneath and partially next to it. There lay the proof of disaster. Amos had stubbornly held out until the last and his folly had cost him dearly. The immense carcass of the animal had crashed down on his head and chest and snuffed out his life.

Even as she checked for signs of a heartbeat, she knew without a doubt that it was too late to do anything for him.

Fresh tears sprang to her eyes. Her father may have been a tyrant but he was still part of her family, part of her life, of Mama's life. And now he was gone. Forever.

As she returned to her mother and youngest sister, Emmeline swiped at her damp cheeks. She was upset with herself for losing control and even more upset with her father for risking all their lives by pressing onward when he knew there was imminent danger.

And, she had to admit, she was also disappointed that her prayers for their safety had not been honored. Why not? Why had God taken Papa from them? Why hadn't Bess and the twins returned to them? And why was Mama trapped?

Realizing that she still had much to be thankful for, Emmeline sobered and sighed. They'd lost one ox, one man and many of their belongings. But she and Mama and Glory and Johnny were still alive and kicking. And Bess and the twins would probably wander back to what was left of their wagon any moment now. Given the severity of the tornado and its accompanying storm, they had probably fared better than many others who had been caught up in the same terrible calamity.

Emmeline cupped her hands around her mouth as she stepped to the edge of the trail where the muddy ruts ended and the grasslands began. "Bess?" she hollered. "Bess? Missy? Mikey? You can come back now!"

To her chagrin, no one answered and no one's head popped up from the beaten-down, thickly matted grasses in the distance.

If she had been sure in which direction to search, Emmeline would have begun to look for them at once. As it was, however, she was so turned around, so disoriented, that she had no earthly idea where to start.

Therefore, her first task had to be to try to free her mother. After that, if Bess wasn't back, she and

Johnny could take turns staying by the wagon or working their way through the soggy vegetation in careful circles until they located the missing children.

Bess and the twins would be fine, Emmeline kept assuring herself.

She just wished she truly believed it was so.

Chapter Three

Will swung by his house, then backtracked to the High Plains settlement as soon as he felt certain his men could manage without him. His home was unscathed, but he was concerned about his friends. And, he was worried about the fate of the wagon train.

He huffed in self-disgust. Who was he kidding? It wasn't the whole train he cared especially about, it was the young woman he'd met mere hours ago. He wanted to believe that her strength and spirit would ensure her safety, but he knew that wasn't the case. It didn't matter how capable or brave a person was, no one had the advantage when caught in a storm the likes of the one that had just passed over the area.

Groves of trees had been mowed down in a narrow swath leading directly to town. As he rode nearer he was flabbergasted by the damage to the buildings, too, not to mention the destruction of the less substantial tents and shacks along the river that had not yet been replaced by more sturdy construction. Many of those were not merely damaged, they were gone! Will paused to murmur a brief prayer for the new settlers. He hoped they had all found a safe place to weather the storm.

Judging by the brave souls who were out and about, picking through the rubble and surveying the destruction, most had taken shelter in time.

He paused to ask the closest survivors, "How is everybody?" and was relieved to hear that there had been no deaths reported, as yet.

The town hall, of which they had all been so proud, had been leveled as well, leaving nothing but the limestone rock foundation. Part of the roof was also off Pete Benjamin's blacksmith shop and it appeared that some of the substantial stores along Main had been hard hit.

Will cantered upriver, in the direction of Zeb's mill, slowing to allow his horse to choose its footing carefully in view of the debris. An amazing amount of refuse littered wide Main Street and it got worse along the narrower Mill Road that led west, toward the falls. There, although many of the trees still stood, they were missing their tops and their remaining branches held all sorts of rubbish, as if a giant, malevolent hand had discarded it there.

He passed a small group of wagons, also tattered and wrecked, before he encountered his old friend, hoofing it into town. "Zeb? You okay?" Will shouted, quickly dismounting to join him.

To his relief, Zeb answered in the affirmative. He had a slightly bloody handkerchief pressed to one temple and his clothes were filthy, but he seemed otherwise unscathed.

"I've been better," Zeb said, dusting off his trousers with his free hand. "The mill's a mess. I don't think there's even one shingle left, not to mention the heavier lumber. How about you?"

"My house made it and the rest of the Circle-L is fine, too, along with all the hands, thank the Lord. We headed off a stampede and kept the buffalo at bay. It was close though."

"Sounds like you did better than we did," Zeb said, grimacing and gesturing at the destruction all around him. "Look at this. It's unbelievable."

"Nothing that can't be fixed," Will told him, "as long as all the folks are okay. How about your sister?"

"Cassandra's fine, thanks."

"Good. Has anybody checked Pete's? The livery stable didn't look too good when I rode past. I didn't see any sign of him or his farrier, Edward."

"I'm going to organize a search party to cover everyone's place and make sure they're alive and kicking. What are you going to do now, go back to your spread or stay here and help us?"

Hesitating, Will was reluctant to admit what was nagging at his conscience. "I'll help, of course. But first, I thought I might ride out and see how that wagon camp is faring."

"Some of them pulled out before the storm. I warned them, but…"

Will muttered under his breath. "I can't believe it. What was their wagon boss thinking? Didn't he see the signs in the changing weather?"

"I wouldn't worry. They probably didn't get far," Zeb said. "But you know settlers. They're all alike. Once they get it into their heads that they have to press on, there's no reasoning with them." He paused and sighed. "Can't tell about the ones who left. The ones that tarried certainly didn't escape damage."

"Did you happen to notice a wagon with a real pretty older daughter? She had blue eyes and a dress to match, and dark hair." He blushed when his friend waggled his eyebrows and stared at him.

Zeb chuckled. "If I didn't know you the way I do, Will Logan, I might think you were interested in her in a personal way. I thought you were looking for a widow woman with older children who just needed a home and hearth, not a swain."

"I didn't say I was going to *court* the girl," Will said flatly. "But her father is a nasty old man, a lot like mine was, and she was having to take care of a wagonload of children, including some that weren't her kin. It's perfectly natural that I'd be concerned for my fellow man."

"Yes," Zeb said, "it is. Except in this instance, your fellow *man* is a *woman*."

"As if I didn't know that." Fisting his reins, Will put his left foot in the stirrup, grabbed the horn and vaulted easily into the saddle. "How long ago did the first wagons in the train pull out?"

"About two hours, I think. I remember that the sky was already darkening when they passed by."

"All right. I'll head down the trail and see how they're doing, then come back and help you here."

"Be careful," Zeb warned. "Just because the worst seems to be over doesn't mean it can't fire up and hit us again."

Will knew he was right. And that thought gave him chills all the way from his nape to the toes of his boots.

Not only had the wagons been in danger before, they could be again. Soon. Perhaps even before he managed to reach them.

Hoping against hope that someone from the rest of their train would ride ahead to check on their welfare, Emmeline kept scanning the trail and surrounding hills. When she spotted several riders silhouetted against the gray sky, she was at first encouraged. Then, she realized that the stationary men, watching from the backs of their horses, were Indians!

Her hand flew to her throat. She didn't know what tribe they were from, nor did she care. The few Indian women she had noticed, in or near small towns along the trail, had seemed wary, almost afraid. She fully understood their reactions. The Indians were outnumbered and vulnerable in that particular situation. And now that she and what remained of her family were stranded in the middle of nowhere, that was exactly how she felt, too.

As she and Johnny prepared to put their shoulders to the side of the wagon to try to move it, Joanna kept insisting that they wait. "Don't try to push that over by yourselves. You're not strong enough. Do as I told you. Get your papa. He'll know what to do."

Emmeline didn't want to inform her that Amos was dead, yet what choice did she have when her mother kept insisting? "Papa's…Papa's not able," she said, hugging Glory and speaking through one of the cracks in the upended wagon.

Joanna gasped audibly. "Dear Lord. Why not? Is he hurt?"

"Yes," Emmeline said.

"Then you should be tending to him. Go. Do it now. I'm fine. Really. I'm not injured a bit and I can wait as long as need be."

Emmeline's voice broke as she forced herself to explain. Reality was almost too terrible to voice. "Papa's gone to heaven, Mama."

"No! No, that can't be. He's just hurt. You'll see. Go look again. You must be mistaken."

"When the wagon turned over, an ox fell on him.

Big Jack is okay but Sam is dead. And Papa's under-
neath him."

"Get him off. Save your father."

"It's too late." Emmeline was fighting tears and
so was her brother. "By—by the time I reached him
to check, he was already getting cold."

Joanna began to wail incoherently. Glory sobbed
softly. And Johnny gritted his teeth while Emmeline
struggled to stay strong for the sake of the others.

"Mama, listen. We'll try to push the wagon over
enough for you to crawl out," she shouted above her
mother's loud, heartbreaking sobs.

Setting Glory out of the way, she motioned to
Johnny and got into place beside him. "On the count
of three. One, two, *three*."

They pushed with all their might but to no avail,
which Emmeline quickly realized was a blessing.
Even if they could have managed to raise the side
of the wagon a little, there was no way to keep it
stable and guarantee that it wouldn't drop and crush
their poor mother during her escape attempt, the
way the ox had done to Papa.

Exhausted, Emmeline shook her head, stood
back and addressed her brother. "Stop. Mama was
right. We aren't strong enough to do this alone."

"No!" the boy insisted. "I can do it."

She knew the helplessness he was feeling and
sympathized. That didn't, however, change facts.
Touching his thin arm, Emmeline stopped him physi-

cally. "We'll get her out. I promise. Only we have to think, not just try harder. There are some things that are beyond us. Let's pray for help to come."

He jerked his arm away and glared at her with reddened, puffy eyes. "That doesn't work." His glance darted toward the place where their father still lay. "I prayed for Papa and look what happened." Emmeline flinched as she heard her brother voice her own doubts. Her prayers hadn't been heeded either. Why?

"Was…was it quick?" Emmeline asked, needing to know yet not wanting to hear that her father had suffered.

Sniffling and wiping his nose on his sleeve, the young teen choked back a sob before answering. "I don't know. When I woke up, Big Jack was standing over me and there was Papa, already so still. I tried to wake him, to pull him free, but…" Johnny stifled another shaky moan. Tears streaked his cheeks.

Touched, Emmeline enfolded him in her arms and held him while he wept on her shoulder. It had been years since the boy had permitted her to show him any affection and their shared hug reminded her of the closer sibling relationship they had once enjoyed. In truth, she'd missed the sweet child her brother had been before he'd grown up enough to begin to emulate their father.

When Johnny finally pushed her away, Emmeline was chagrined. She truly loved the members of her family, all of them, even though they were sometimes less than lovable.

Swiping at his damp cheeks, Johnny pointed east, up the trail. "Look!"

At first, Emmeline feared that the distant Indians had decided to approach. Then, she realized that the horseman was riding with saddle and bridle as well as wearing a slicker that flapped out behind him like great, black wings. No Indian would ride or dress like that, at least not any she had seen thus far in her travels.

She held up her arms, waved boldly and shouted to the rider. "Over here. Hurry! We need help."

He slid off his mount and started to run toward her before the horse had come to a complete stop.

She *knew* that man. *Glory be!* It was the cowboy from the mercantile. And no one had ever looked better to her, not even erstwhile beaus from her old hometown.

Unable to recall his name, she nevertheless greeted him with unbounded enthusiasm. Clasping her hands, she shouted, "Hallelujah!"

"What's happened? Are you all right?"

"Some of us are," Emmeline answered, sobering and glancing over her shoulder toward the place where the remains of the ox still lay. "The important thing right now is rescuing my mother. She's trapped under the wagon. Johnny and I tried to lift it but it was too heavy."

Will was fetching his rope from where it was tied at the fork of his saddle. "Where's your father? We'll need all the muscle we can get."

Emmeline lowered her voice. "Papa will not be helping. He's gone to meet his Maker."

The cowboy merely nodded and went to work instead of asking for further explanation.

Relieved, Emmeline sighed. There was really nothing else to say. And now that a friend had arrived to help, she finally had a moment to step back and take stock of the situation. It wasn't a pretty picture. When the last breath had left her father's body, their whole life had changed. They had no home, no money to speak of, very few possessions and no predictable future. She didn't know how things could get any worse.

And then she remembered that Bess and the twins were still missing.

Will had formally introduced himself to Johnny while he threaded his rope through two of the wagon wheels on the off side. Then, he and the boy used his horse in tandem with the surviving ox to pull.

The rope held. The wagon creaked and groaned as it tilted onto its side. It wobbled for a moment, then settled there in the soft mud, as stable as could be expected, considering the rutted ground.

He watched the tearful reunion of mother and

daughters, noting that Johnny stood back with the ox and made no effort to join them.

"Help me free my rope, will you?" Will asked the boy. At first he thought Johnny had not heard. Then, the wiry youngster clambered atop the wagon to assist him.

"Appreciate it," Will said, coiling the stiff, braided rawhide as he spoke.

Still, the boy did not reply. He seemed to be fixated on the dead ox, so Will started to approach it.

Johnny broke into a run and dashed past. "Don't touch him. Don't you dare touch him."

In moments, Will took in the entire picture and understood everything. He gently patted the man-child's thin shoulder. "Somebody will have to do it, son. You don't want your ma and sisters to see him this way, do you?"

There was no answer, yet Will could feel the youngster's shoulders slumping and see the slight shake of his head.

"Then go fetch me a cover. Not your mama's nice things. Bring something old that she won't mind losing. When we're ready, I'll use my horse to pull the critter aside and you can cover your pa yourself if that's what you want to do."

Staring at Amos's remains while he waited for the boy to return, Will thought of his own father and the last time he'd seen him alive. He'd been drunk, as usual. And as mean as a snake. Also his normal state. Perhaps it wasn't fair to paint this man as the same kind of villain, but he'd heard him speaking about his wife and children in the mercantile and his words had been anything but kind.

Johnny hurried back and displayed a soggy blanket for Will's approval. "That's—that's all I can find that didn't blow away. Mama wants to come see, but Emmeline is stopping her. We'd better hurry."

Emmeline? So, that was the eldest girl's name. Pretty. And fitting, he guessed, although if he'd been naming her he might have chosen something a tad less pretentious.

Shaking himself to clear his head and concentrate on the necessary task at hand, he looped his rope over the ox's horns, mounted his horse and used it to tow the animal a few yards. Part of the man's body was pressed into the mud as if it were barely there and the boy was tenderly covering it.

What was this poor family going to do now? Will wondered. *What, indeed?* He supposed they could try to find another team and keep heading west, but not without at least one drover, not to mention someone who could also hunt to add wild game to their victuals. The laying hens that might have survived the tornado were long gone into the tall grass, and nobody could manage with only one ox. Plus, most of their larder, such as flour and beans and bacon, had been lost or ruined when their wagon had tipped over. The box was cracked and every bow that had held up the canvas cover—which was missing—had been smashed to smithereens. If they had money it might be easiest to give up their own wagon and pay for space in another family's…but Will doubted they had enough funds for that, even if anyone could be found with room to spare.

He was about to inform the women that it was safe to look at the place where the man lay, when Emmeline approached him. He dismounted to speak with her and removed his hat while her mother fell to her knees beside the older man's body, rocking and keening disconsolately.

Emmeline offered her small hand and Will took and held it for a brief moment.

"I would like to thank you for everything you've done, Mr.—" she began, finally adding, "—forgive me. I don't seem to recall your name."

"It's Will Logan."

"Then thank you, Mr. Logan." Withdrawing, she folded her arms across her chest to pull her shawl closer. She was still dripping wet and clearly shivering. He took off his slicker and handed it to her.

She accepted the gift graciously. "Thank you. My mother will need this. I have no earthly idea where most of our belongings ended up. They're not in the wagon anymore."

Although she was handling herself well at the moment, Will could tell she was suffering and he didn't know what to say or do to help her further.

When she continued speaking, however, he realized that the family's predicament was far from over.

"My, my sister Bess and the twins are missing," Emmeline said haltingly. "It's all my fault. I sent them off the trail to look for shelter and now I don't know where they are."

Will was thunderstruck. He supposed he should have missed the others right away, but in all the confusion following the upset wagon he'd not thought of anything else. "Where did you see them last?" he asked.

Unshed tears filled the young woman's eyes, deepening their blue color. "I'm not certain. I think it was back twenty or thirty feet where Papa first stopped the wagon. When they ran off it was opposite the direction the terrible wind was coming from."

"Then they went northeast," Will said, mounting up. "I'll start looking in that direction. You stay here with your mother. I came past part of your train about two miles back. They said they'd head this way to check on you just as soon as they'd rounded up some livestock that stampeded in the storm."

"We *have* to find Bess and those poor little tykes," Emmeline said, her voice breaking. "Please, please find them, sir."

"I'll do my best," Will told her. He reined his excited horse in a tight circle to keep it from racing off before he was ready. "Looking for their trail after the grass has been so flattened will be difficult, but I'll give it a try. If I'm not back by the time more help arrives, tell them where I've gone and have them start a more careful search."

He paused, then decided to say all that was on his mind. "And don't get caught out in the prairie alone, Miss Emmeline. The local Indians are friendly enough, under the right circumstances, but they can't be trusted."

Her eyes widened. "I saw some." She pointed. "They were over there. On that ridge."

"Watching for a chance to help themselves to whatever you leave behind, I reckon," Will said. "They don't usually steal brazenly, but they aren't averse to picking up the spoils."

"What about my sister? Bess is only fifteen."

Nodding, Will knew he had to be truthful for the young woman's own protection, yet he was loath to frighten her unnecessarily. "If she keeps her wits about her, she won't be harmed," he said, only half believing it.

In his heart, he wished mightily that the missing girl was a lot younger, like the orphan twins with her, so that if she was captured she'd be treated as a member of the Indians' families, rather than as a slave.

He gritted his teeth. *Or as a potential bride.*

Chapter Four

For Emmeline, the waiting and standing helplessly idle were hard to bear. She began to salvage household items that were close at hand and pile them next to the wagon box as she watched Will riding in ever-widening arcs away from the main trail. The country was so vast, so untamed, it seemed as if his task was insurmountable.

She was relieved to note that the distant Indians had apparently gone away. That was something to count as a blessing, at least. If only Mama wasn't so downtrodden. Emmeline was grown, yes, but she still would have welcomed someone else being able to share some of the responsibility for her family's welfare, even if that provided her only a few minutes' respite.

Looking back along the rutted trail that had brought them to this place, she kept expecting to glimpse the aid Will had assured her was on its way. So far, there had been no sign of other settlers or their wagons. If they had experienced the storm at even half the strength that she and her kin had, there was no telling when they would be moving forward again.

Will finished another sweep through the tall grasses, then returned to where Emmeline waited with the stack of soggy bedding and other salvaged items.

"Did you see any sign of them?" she asked, knowing what his answer would be from his grave countenance.

He bent in his saddle to speak quietly with her. "No. How is your mother faring?"

"Not well, I'm afraid. Glory is so sweet the way she's trying to cheer her, though Johnny is his usual moody self. But Mama has been weeping ever since she heard what happened to Papa. She just keeps sitting there and calling his name, over and over again."

"That's understandable. She's had a bad shock. Do you want to stay here with her?"

"Or do what?" Emmeline asked.

"I thought, if there were two of us looking, we might have a better chance of spotting your sister."

"You told me to avoid going out alone."

"Yes, I did."

Although the sky was still cloudy and his hat brim shaded his ruggedly handsome face, Emmeline was positive she could see his cheeks grow rosy. That led her to ask, "Are you suggesting that we *both* ride your horse?"

"I apologize," Will replied. "I realize that a good Christian lady like you—-"

"You're right. Normally I wouldn't consider riding double with you. But my sister and two helpless little children are missing. I'm not the kind of person to stand on etiquette if my actions might save them from whatever dangers lie out there."

"All right. Go tell the others what we're going to do and let's head out again. It'll be dark in another few hours. Time's a-wasting."

She knew he was right. More than right. He had to be downplaying the imminent danger to Bess and to everyone else. The sooner they located the lost members of her party and rejoined the larger group from the wagon train, the safer everyone would be.

It immediately struck Emmeline that their place in the westward-bound convoy would probably remain empty when the rest of the pioneers reassembled and pressed on. She could not hope to ready their damaged wagon and find a new team in time to go along, nor could she make other plans— not until they'd found Bess, Missy and Mikey.

If they found them.

Waiting aside, Will watched as Emmeline spoke quietly with the surviving members of her family. No one had yet asked about arranging burial for

Amos, but he knew that subject would soon arise. There was a small cemetery on the outskirts of High Plains, next to the community church. The blacksmith's wife, Sarah, and their newborn child had been the first interred there, much to everyone's sorrow, but they hadn't been the last. Still, there would be room for Amos Carter. Will would see to that. The man would have a better resting place than a shallow grave beside the trail, even if that was what many pioneers had been forced to settle for in the past and surely would again. Making the long trek to the new state of Oregon was hazardous, at best. Many dreams had ended in tragedy on that trail, just as this family's had. But for Emmeline's sake, Will would make sure her father had a decent Christian burial.

He urged his horse forward as Emmeline returned. "Did you decide to come with me?"

"Yes."

"Then let's get a move on."

Reaching up, she grasped the wrist of the hand he offered. He easily swung her up to ride behind the cantle of his saddle. It did surprise him a bit that she chose to sit astride, but given the sorry state of her formerly lovely dress, it was certainly not going to harm her clothing to do so.

"All set?" Will asked. Before she answered he felt her slim arms gently slipping around his waist.

"Yes. If you will permit me to hold on."

"As you said, this is no time for us to worry about keeping to etiquette. I certainly won't think poorly of you for doing so, ma'am. And I'm sure your missing sister will agree, too, once we've found her."

He gave the horse a nudge with his heels and started back onto the prairie. By now, some of the beaten-down grasses had recovered and sprung back, making movement a little easier but cutting down on distance visibility.

Even while she was sitting astride the gelding, Will knew that Emmeline would barely be able to see over the tops of the big bluestem once it was back to its full height. By late summer, some of that prairie grass would reach a height of ten feet or more. It was great fodder for his cattle and the wild buffalo. It just wasn't an ideal place for conducting a search.

Will's innate sense of direction stood him in good stead. He knew which ground he had already covered and didn't repeat that path, thereby saving time.

"I forgot to ask. What colors were they wearing?" he inquired, more for something to say than because he needed to know. Given the normal greens and browns of the prairie and the drifts of so many different varieties of blooming wildflowers, spotting unnatural objects lying within the cover of the vegetation would be extremely difficult, no matter what, but any clue could help.

His heart gave an unexpected jolt when his passenger tightened her hold on him and leaned forward to speak past his left shoulder.

"Bess had on a blue calico, like mine," Emmeline said. "I don't remember what the twins were wearing. I suppose Missy was wearing one of Bess's old dresses, and I recall the pink ribbons in her hair. And Mikey always wore Johnny's shirts over breeches that were way too short." Her voice caught for a moment before she recovered and went on. "We used to tease him about being so skinny that his old pants still fit, even if they were practically knee britches by now."

"Okay. Just keep your eyes open. I'm going to head for a bluff nearby in the hopes they found shelter there."

"We didn't know where to go or what to do," Emmeline said. "I suppose I should have pulled everyone into the wagon, but I thought Mama would have sense enough to run away with Glory and me."

"Is that how you ended up outside while your mother was trapped?"

"No."

Will felt her slumping as she eased away, relaxed a little and gave an audible sigh.

"I was in the wagon when the wind picked me up and carried me off," Emmeline said. "Glory, too. The last thing I remember is praying that the baby would be all right. Then, everything went dark."

He reined in. The saddle leather creaked as he swiveled to peer at her over his shoulder. "What? Why didn't you tell me all that before? Are you sure you aren't hurt?"

"As sure as I can be, considering," Emmeline said. "I know I bumped my head, and it was pounding when I woke up, but it seems all right now, and I think that was the worst of it. That, and a few little scratches. If Glory and I had been in that wagon when it flipped over, one or both of us could have been caught halfway out and killed just like Papa was."

The very mention of that possibility gave Will the chills. His simple urge to locate the little family and check on their welfare had not prepared him for finding this lovely young woman injured—or worse. All along, he had been picturing himself arriving to help her, just as he had. Now, when he thought about the chances that she might have been killed, his heart lurched like a frightened pony.

"Well, you weren't badly hurt, so we can give thanks for that," he said, hoping he sounded encouraging instead of the way he was really feeling. The fact that they had found no trace of her sister or the younger children was not a good sign. Not good at all.

He paused on the next hillock to stretch in the saddle, shade his eyes against the glare of the setting sun and scan the lower-lying landscape. "I don't see anything, do you?"

"Just scattered blankets and a few smaller things. Mama's bedding and most of our clothing must have been carried for miles and miles."

"I'll help you gather up more of it later. Right now, first things first."

He was about to turn and take Emmeline back to the Carter wagon when she tightened her hold on his rib cage with one arm, pointed with the other and screeched, "Stop!" frightening the horse enough to cause it to jump and prance sideways, almost unseating them both.

Will jerked back on the reins and managed to quiet the fractious horse and regain control before he asked, "What's wrong?"

"Over there!" she shouted. "See that blue fabric? It looks like Bess's dress!"

In Emmeline's opinion, reaching the prostrate form of her poor sister was taking an eternity. She kept kicking the horse in the flanks while Will held it in check with a tight rein.

"Faster!" she insisted. "Either hurry up or let me off right here."

"If we gallop and the little ones are lying in the grass where we can't see them, it'll just make matters worse. Settle down. We're almost there."

She knew he was right, but that didn't make it

any easier to bide her time. Patience had never been one of her virtues and being embroiled in this tragedy had not helped one iota.

If anything, it had made her more anxious. That was not something she considered a fault or a sin. On the contrary, she thought she was doing well to keep from screaming at the poor man whom she knew was merely trying to help.

"Bess!" Emmeline called. "Bess, I'm here. I'm coming."

The figure lying prostrate on a patch of rocky ground did not stir.

As Will reined in beside it, Emmeline pushed herself back, slid over the horse's rear and dropped to the ground. She was already kneeling at her sister's side and shaking the girl's shoulders when Will joined her.

"Is she alive?" he asked.

"Yes, she's breathing, thank the Lord. I don't know why she doesn't wake up."

"Don't be too rough with her," he warned. "She might have broken bones."

"It's my fault, it's all my fault," Emmeline keened as tears slipped down her cheeks and fell to bathe her sister's face.

"You didn't make the bad weather and you weren't responsible for your father's decision to press on," he countered.

Then it must be God's fault for not looking after

us, she thought so quickly, so instinctively that she was unable to censor it. Instead of voicing that disturbing conclusion, she said, "Bess doesn't deserve this. She's never hurt a fly."

Will had been studying the area around them. He bent and hefted a portion of a large tree limb that lay a few yards away. "I think this is what may have hit your sister in the head and knocked her out. Check in her hair and see if there's a lump."

Following his instructions, Emmeline found one small wound at Bess's temple and a welt on the back of her head. "Yes. There's a goose egg and…" She cradled the girl's head and shoulders and was about to continue searching for further injuries, when the younger girl stirred.

"Bess? Dear? It's Emmeline. You're safe now."

Her sister's eyelashes fluttered. Grinning while shedding tears of relief and thankfulness, Emmeline looked to Will. "I think—"

"Yes. She's coming around." He crouched next to them.

When Bess's eyes opened and focused on Emmeline, she opened her mouth as if to speak. Her eyes widened in apparent terror. Emmeline had thought the girl was going to scream, but no sound came forth. Nor were there tears.

Continuing to cradle her and taking her hand, Emmeline patted it gently, reassuringly. "It's all right, Bess. I'm here. You're going to be fine."

The fifteen-year-old seemed to relax some, but made no reply.

"I have a friend here with a horse. We'll take you back to the wagon just as soon as we locate Missy and Mikey," Emmeline explained. "Where are they? Did you all find a place to hunker down?"

Receiving not the slightest nod, let alone a lucid answer, she was beginning to grow terribly concerned. She glanced at Will. "I don't understand what's wrong with her. Could a bump on the head cause her to lose her voice?"

"It's more likely that she's just had the sense knocked out of her," he replied, frowning. He got to his feet and studied the surrounding prairie. "You stay with her for a few minutes and try to get her to talk to you. I'll ride out a bit more and see if the younger ones are close by."

Emmeline redirected her attention to her ailing sister and wiped some of the mud off her cheeks with a damp scrap of petticoat. "Bess? Please? You're frightening me."

The younger girl simply stared as if not truly seeing anything or anyone.

Emmeline had never been around a person who looked or acted so emotionally disconnected. Surely Bess would recover soon, she thought. She had to. And she'd be able to tell them where to find the missing twins. But until then...

Maybe the helpful rancher will come across

them, Emmeline told herself, only half believing that rationale. It was amazing that they had stumbled upon Bess out there in the midst of that sea of tall grass. Finding smaller targets was going to be next to impossible.

Emmeline hugged her sister and held her close for shared warmth while they waited for Will Logan to return. The sun was lowering in the west, bringing a chill that was aggravated by the fact that their clothing was still soaked and the wind had begun to blow again.

Struggling to remain calm and keep her wits about her, Emmeline was struck by the fact that she had never felt so lost, so helpless, in all her nineteen years on this earth.

Will experienced several instances in which he'd actually thought he'd located the lost children. Unfortunately, he was merely seeing additional refuse from the destruction of the Carter wagon, and probably from others, as well.

Household trappings were strewn across the flint hills for miles. He had begun gathering up what he thought were the possessions belonging to Emmeline's family but had quickly concluded that that was a chore better done by a group of people, preferably womenfolk, considering some of the feminine garments he was finding.

As he made his way back to where Emmeline

and her sister waited, he wished he had better news for them. It looked as though those orphaned children had disappeared from the face of the earth, leaving no trace.

That was impossible, of course, yet Will knew all too well that they could have met with disaster in more ways than one. If the tornado had not ended their lives and they were not wandering the prairie lost, hungry and freezing, perhaps they were being held captive by Indians.

He knew that the Kansa, the "Wind People," were basically peaceful under most circumstances, but they'd been pushed hard of late, losing land to the machinations of the federal government and the cheating of greedy land-grabbers. Given that unfair treatment, the lack of enough to eat last winter and repeated epidemics of cholera and other diseases, even the most amiable tribes would have been up in arms. That the whole area had not already erupted in war between the settlers and natives was a credit to both sides. Will didn't think the Indians would harm children…but if they found the twins, they wouldn't be in any hurry to bring them back.

Emmeline scrambled to her feet as soon as Will approached. Their gazes met. "Did you find any sign of them?"

"No." He shook his head sadly. "I think we should get your sister back to civilization and have a doctor look at her. There's an old medical man in High

Plains. Doc Dempsey's not much, but he's bound to know more about what ails her than you and I do."

"I'm not leaving here without the twins."

Will had figured she'd argue and was ready with a rational reply. "There are plenty of other folks who can scour these plains for the children. You're the one your family needs to take charge right now. I can tell that your mama's not able. There's no one else, is there?"

"No." She shook her head. "I suppose there isn't."

"Then it's up to you to see to everyone's needs. I'll help you however you say."

"Unless you happen to disagree with me?"

That comment brought a slight smile in spite of Will's determination to continue to treat the young woman's concerns with the utmost seriousness. That she would say something so wryly clever at a time like this spoke well of her. She was obviously more resilient and emotionally well balanced in the face of this crisis than the rest of her family, thank the good Lord. If Emmeline Carter had fallen apart the way her mother and siblings had, there would be little hope for their future.

And speaking of the future…"Do you think you can steady your sister in the saddle while we go back to get your mother?"

"Of course. But once we get there what about Mama and Glory? They can't all ride your poor horse into town."

"Some of us can walk, and we'll take turns until we meet up with more folks and get some help. We're not very far from High Plains, as the crow flies."

He made a step for Emmeline by lacing his fingers together, and gave her a boost to assist her in mounting. Then, he gently guided Bess into place, lifted her with his hands on her waist and placed her sidesaddle in Emmeline's lap. The girl was still not responding normally, but she did seem willing to ride without protest, much to Will's relief.

He fisted the reins and stepped back, preparing to lead. "All set?"

"Yes," Emmeline said firmly.

Will's admiration for the young woman blossomed with each moment, each word, each selfless act. She had to be scared and cold and probably terribly sore from the tumble the wind had given her, yet she sat as tall and brave astride that horse as any man he'd ever known, shielding her sister with obvious care.

As he led the horse back toward the scene of the wagon wreck, Will turned his thoughts heavenward and offered a silent prayer for Emmeline and her loved ones. She was going to need plenty of help in the coming days and weeks. He would do all he could, of course, and he knew other citizens of High Plains would also come to her aid.

He also knew, without a doubt, that the best efforts of men were going to fall short. The Carter family was in dire straits and would remain so for the foreseeable future. In Will's opinion, their only real hope was divine intervention.

Chapter Five

Emmeline's mind was made up. There was no way she was going to leave High Plains until they had located the twins. Rather than argue with anyone about it, she chose to keep her decision to herself for the present.

She had spent her whole life obeying her father, and look what that attitude of submission had led to. They were stranded in the territories, helpless and practically penniless, with one member of their party deceased, two missing and the rest barely functional. In her opinion, it was high time for a leadership change. She was taking over.

She let Will assist Bess in dismounting and watched the reunion between the girl and their tearful mother. Sadly, Emmeline overheard no spoken words from Bess. She had hoped that returning her sister to the wagon would bring her to her senses, but, that had not happened.

She swung her right leg over the saddle, kicked free of the stirrup and let herself slide to the ground before Will could offer assistance.

"Please put Mama on the horse with Bess and Glory and take them to town," Emmeline ordered. "Johnny and I will tarry here until others from the train arrive. They can help us salvage the wagon, if possible, and loan us an ox to pull beside ours so we can bring everything."

"No. Possessions don't matter at this point. You're all coming with me."

Emmeline huffed and faced him, hands on her hips. "I beg your pardon?"

"You heard me. You need to think of your sister and the others. They need you. And they also need to be spirited away from this wreck as soon as possible. You know that."

"Okay. Maybe. What, exactly, did you have in mind?"

"I'll take you and your family into town while others stay behind and continue searching."

"I should be the one to do the looking because it's my fault they were lost. Johnny can stay with me while you take Mama, Bess and Glory to the doctor."

"And how will you and your brother defend yourselves if the Indians return?"

Not having recovered either her father's rifle or

his shotgun, so far, Emmeline stifled a shiver. "The Indians are long gone. You said so yourself."

"Now, they are. What's to say they won't return at dark? I would if I were them."

"And steal all we have left," Emmeline added. "My family had little to start with, but whatever we can salvage, we will surely need, even if it isn't much."

She could tell she was gaining his confidence when he nodded and capitulated.

"All right. If no one else shows up in a few more minutes, I'll ride back and fetch some folks from the wagon train's company."

"Now, *that* makes sense."

"Yes, ma'am."

His attitude seemed less one of willing cooperation than of resignation. That would have to suffice. She had few options.

Folding her arms and pulling her damp shawl tighter against the encroaching evening, Emmeline surveyed what was left of her former life. Her heart sank. She was finally in control of her own destiny, but she had so little left, it was almost laughable.

Sweet Jesus, what am I going to do? she thought prayerfully. *How are we all going to survive, let alone prosper? Help us? Please? Tell me what course to follow?*

No booming voice split the gray heavens, nor did she receive a stunning mental revelation. She did, however, begin to realize that the rancher who had befriended her was part of the answer to her heart-felt plea. They had become acquainted before she had known she'd need help and he had subsequently offered aid when it was desperately needed.

And I spoke too harshly to him, Emmeline reminded herself, mortified. That was an unkindness she must put right immediately.

"Mr. Logan," she said, lightly tapping his arm for emphasis and to be sure she had his full attention. "I want to apologize for my attitude. When I should have been thanking you for coming to our rescue, I spoke thoughtlessly. Please forgive me?"

His surprised expression was so amusing she might have laughed had they been caught up in less trying circumstances.

"I see no reason to apologize," Will said. "You have just been through some terrible trials."

Emmeline nodded. "True. And they are far from over." She eyed her mother who had drawn Glory into her embrace while Bess stood aside and Johnny continued to tend to the surviving ox. "It has occurred to me that I shall also need to make arrangements for my father's burial. Can you assist me with that?"

"Yes. There's a small cemetery in High Plains, near the church. Our Reverend Preston can say a few words over him, if you'd like."

Sighing, Emmeline agreed. "I suppose every man deserves that. And it will give Mama peace to hear such things."

"That's all any of us can ask," Will said wisely. "From what I observed in the mercantile, my late father was a lot like yours."

As her eyes met his, she realized that there was true empathy in his clear blue gaze. He did understand. And he wasn't holding it against her that she was not weeping for Amos or lamenting his passing the way her mother was.

Perhaps that was odd, even wrong, yet when Emmeline searched her heart she found mostly sad relief in regard to her father's demise. Was it sinful to be comforted by the knowledge that they would no longer have to fear the man's volatile temper or wonder who was going to be on the receiving end of his wrath the next time he got upset over some trifle?

No, she decided easily. This tragedy may have placed them in dire straits, but it had also served to rescue them all from the cruel domination of a man who was not fit to be a husband or father to anyone. Why Mama had been so blind to his faults and had married him in the first place, let alone stayed in such a terrible marriage all those years while permitting herself and her children to be abused, was beyond Emmeline's understanding.

One thing was clear. She was never going to make that kind of mistake. No man was ever going to lord it over her. She didn't know how she was going to survive or how she was going to take care of Mama and the others, but she would manage. Somehow. And no man would control their family again. She vowed that with all her heart and soul.

Will saw a small party of horsemen approaching and thought it best to ride out to meet them and advise them of the details before they arrived at the wreck and inadvertently said the wrong things.

He stopped his sorrel sideways to block their path. Some of the riders he recognized from town, while others were obviously from the wagon-train party.

"The Carter wagon, up ahead, has suffered greatly," Will told the group's middle-aged leader. "The head of the family has been killed and two small children are still missing."

Nodding soberly, the older man turned and relayed the message to the others close by. Most of the men took the bad news with evident concern as it filtered to the rear of the group. Back there, however, a few of the younger men seemed to be treating their mission as a lark, hooting and slapping each other on the back as if they were about to attend a picnic instead of a wake.

Will frowned and gestured. "I recognize some of your party as being from High Plains. Who are those three other riders, the ones who think this mess is funny?"

"They're just the Tully brothers. Pay them no mind. They're big, but they ain't too bright."

"Forgive me for saying so, but do you think they'll help and not hinder our efforts?"

"Can't rightly say," the leader replied. "I figured it was best to let them come rather than argue and start a fight. Just ignore 'em. They're harmless if you don't pay them much mind."

"All right. Whatever you say. Let's get started then. I'll show you where I've already searched and you can send small groups out in a pattern to continue looking."

Wheeling his horse, Will led the rescuers back to the damaged wagon. He needed all the eyes he could muster to look for the lost children. Even if the Tullys weren't duly empathetic, that didn't mean they wouldn't be useful in an organized search. Every community had folks like that, ones who were so self-centered that they turned his stomach or made him angry. Or both. But he wouldn't let his aggravation with them distract him from what needed to be done.

This situation called for cool heads and firm leadership decisions, Will kept telling himself. That much he could offer. Whether Miss Emmeline Carter chose to accept his efforts or balk, he was still going to take charge and see that every inch of prairie was explored. Those lost little ones had to be out there. Somewhere. And by the grace of God, he'd find them and bring them back to her. But the missing twins weren't the only obstacle the Carters faced. Providing for themselves would be a challenge.

The way Will had it figured, all he had to do was convince the women that their place was in High Plains where they could be properly cared for. And from what he'd seen of Emmeline's stubbornness, he knew that would have been well nigh impossible if Bess had not been in clear need of medical attention.

Emmeline had been pacing, shading her eyes and staring at the open plains as the others fanned out and began to search.

"We should go pretty soon," Will told her for the third time.

"Just a little longer. Please? Surely the search parties will find the twins soon."

"Of course they will. And as soon as they do, they'll bring them into town," he countered. "Like I said, need to think of your sisters and your mother. It will be dark soon. They'll be chilled to the bone as soon as the sun goes down. Surely, you can see that."

"Yes, but—"

"No buts about it. Johnny can stay here with the men, if you want, while you and I escort the others into High Plains. It suffered some damage, too, but the church was unscathed. That's where I imagine most folks will gather."

"You say there's a doctor there who can look after Bess?" Emmeline asked.

"Yes."

Will knew he should have explained that the town doctor was elderly and about as incompetent as anyone in that profession could be, but he didn't want to discourage compliance with his plans. Zeb had been trying to recruit a replacement medical man ever since the death of Pete's wife and baby, but so far to no avail. Therefore, for the present, they were allowing Dr. Dempsey to muddle through, and were augmenting his so-called expertise with common sense and home remedies.

"I'll tell the men standing guard over your father what we're going to do, see if I can borrow a second horse and then we'll leave. As soon as they have a suitable conveyance, they can bring your father into town, too."

She hesitated. Then, to Will's relief, she nodded. "All right. Do it. I'll get Mama and my sisters ready to travel."

For Emmeline, the notion of walking away from the last remnants of her previous life was hard to accept. She felt as if she was taking part in a sorrowful pageant of some sort rather than experiencing reality. Even when she put her arm around her mother's shaking shoulders and led her from her mourning place, she couldn't believe she was doing so. Nor could she recall much about the short ride back to High Plains.

Her eyes widened when they drew close enough to see all the damage to the once-lovely little town. What a shame. There were many trees either uprooted or fractured in two. Parts of roofs, walls and shingles littered the muddy, rutted street. Fabric that had most likely been pretty curtains that very morning was festooned from broken tree branches and flapping like tattered flags in what remained of the prairie wind.

Knots of people had gathered on Main Street in front of Johnson's mercantile. Some were loudly discussing temporary living arrangements while others milled around like motherless calves after a blizzard.

"I think we should go straight to the church," Will told Emmeline. "I imagine the doctor is pretty busy, but I want him to take a look at your sister as soon as possible."

"I agree," she said, glancing at her mother, Bess and little Glory, wrapped in a blanket and seated atop the extra horse while she rode behind the rancher once again. "Mama probably needs attention, too. I've never seen her look so drawn."

"She wore herself out," Will said. "Time will heal most of what ails her. I'm afraid Bess may be another story."

"I wish you were wrong," Emmeline replied, "but I fear you are all too correct." She kept scanning the crowd. "I had hoped that maybe someone else had found the twins and brought them into town."

"I hadn't considered that, but it is a possibility. I'll pass the word and have some friends ask around. High Plains isn't so big that they'd go unnoticed for long."

"If only Papa had remained with the rest of the wagon train when it stopped to wait out the storm. I tried to tell him it was going to be a bad storm, but even I had no idea *how* bad."

"None of us did. And it might not have made much difference. Some of the wagons at the other end of your train were damaged, too."

Slowing the horse, Will swung his right leg over the saddle horn and jumped down without unseating Emmeline. She watched him wave and call to a dirty but otherwise well-turned-out gentleman in the crowd. "Hey, Zeb! Where's the doc? Have you seen him lately?"

The man jogged over to Will and their bedraggled little party, grasped his hand and pumped it with enthusiasm. "You made it back. Thank the Lord. I was getting worried."

Will stood to one side and gestured. "Zeb Garrison, I'd like you to meet Miss Emmeline Carter, her mother and sisters. Their wagon was turned over and one member of their party lost. Her brother and some settlers should be bringing him into town soon."

"My sincere sympathy, ladies," Zeb said, removing his hat and making a slight bow as he addressed Emmeline primarily. "If there is anything I can do for you, just ask. Right now, we're providing for everyone at the church. Later, when you're ready, we have a blacksmith who's also an excellent wheelwright. His shop was damaged in the storm, but I know he can have your wagon serviceable in short order, once he's back in business."

Emmeline leaned down to offer her hand. "Thank you, sir. Right now, that is the least of my worries." She gestured at those mounted on the other horse. "My mother is ill, my sister Bess has been injured and our party is missing two eight-year-old children. Has there been any sign of them here?"

"Sorry. Not that I've heard," Zeb said.

"I left some of the men from the train searching the area where they were last seen," Will explained as he led both horses down the center of the street and continued to speak with his friend. "After I get these ladies to the church and see if I can locate the doctor, I'm heading back out to keep looking, too."

"We'll organize another search party from here as soon as we're sure nobody's seen them," Zeb offered quickly. "Will, you'll need to lead it so we'll know exactly where to start."

"Done." He looped the horses' reins over a hitching post in front of the large church.

Emmeline slid to the ground without help and reached for Glory. The five-year-old was shivering, as were they all, even though Mrs. Carter had donned Will's slicker and had tucked the little girl beneath it and the blanket to hold her close.

"Take your little sister into the church," he told Emmeline. "We'll bring the others."

Her first instinct was to tarry, to insist she look around town herself, but there was simply no more fight left in her. She was shivering and knew she was approaching exhaustion. Little wonder. She had shepherded her family through a disaster and remained strong for their sakes. No one could have done a better job, yet even she had her limits.

And now what? Emmeline asked herself as she climbed the front steps and entered the immense sanctuary. She supposed that it was wisest to take one minute, one hour, one day at a time, at least until she knew more about Bess and the twins. Perhaps they could find temporary lodging at the boarding-house, she reasoned, although many of the other displaced people would probably be looking to do the same. The place didn't appear spacious enough to accommodate everyone who had had wagons or other possessions damaged during the storm. Besides, if a body didn't have much extra money, staying there might prove a very unwise choice.

Which left either living in their busted wagon or moving in with someone in High Plains. Judging by the destruction she had observed as they had entered town, there wouldn't be many folks equipped to take in boarders who could not pay, let alone provide for their own family's needs.

Raising her eyes to the front of the main sanctuary, Emmeline was reminded of her church back home and had an unexpected sense of déjà vu, of returning to the familiar. Church had always meant being part of a big, loving family, and she suddenly felt more at home than she had at any time since leaving Missouri. This place was well and truly a *sanctuary*.

Will continued to assist Mrs. Carter and Bess while Zeb went off to organize more search parties and put out the word on the missing twins.

Inside the church, Matilda Johnson was already talking to Emmeline and fussing over Glory while her daughter, Abigail, stood back and stared at the new arrivals as if she was observing something distasteful.

She and Emmeline had to be close to the same age, Will thought, yet there was no comparison in their characters. Although the fair-haired Abigail was considered comely by many men, she had a haughty spirit that made Will cringe, especially when she took a notion to smile at him. Unlike Emmeline, there was no warmth in Abigail's eyes, no true kindness in her expression. And right now she was giving poor Emmeline and her kin a look that was pure disapproval, as if the others could help their disheveled condition.

He guided Mrs. Carter, Bess, Emmeline and Glory to an empty bench and urged them to rest while he scanned the crowd for Dr. Dempsey. Since the old man's office, such as it was, had obviously been damaged by the twister, Will had hoped to find him tending new arrivals in the largest building in town.

He wasn't disappointed. "Over here, Doc!" he called, motioning broadly and shouting to be heard over the din inside the cavernous room.

As the elderly man approached, Will noticed that his usual tremors were exaggerated, probably due to the stress of the moment.

"You all right, Will?" he asked, placing his worn black bag on the floor at their feet.

"I am. But these ladies need attention, especially Miss Bess, here. She got hit in the head and she seems pretty groggy."

Dempsey reached for the girl's chin and managed to turn her to face him in spite of his shaking hands. Squinting, he peered into her eyes, then shook his head. "Hysteria, I reckon. A lot of these women are sufferin' from that. I'll give her a dose of laudanum to help her rest tonight. She should be fine in the morning."

Emmeline grasped his bony wrist. "There are two places where she was hurt. We think a limb hit her on the head. Aren't you going to even look at those cuts?"

"Not unless she needs to be sewed up, little lady."

When he followed that statement with a kindly, grandfatherly smile and patted Emmeline on the top of the head, Will was afraid the young woman was going to say something unseemly. There was certainly enough fire in her gaze to herald such an outburst. All she did, however, was inch out of the old man's reach, grit her teeth and hold her peace.

Under less stressful circumstances Will would have laughed aloud. Not only was Emmeline Carter no child, in his opinion she was more driven and determined than most men, including the elderly doctor. She was so muddy and tousled that her hair resembled a wild, prairie rosebush. Those formerly silky locks were tossed and matted, her skirt was tattered and plastered with mud, and the rest of her clothing looked as if it had been plucked from a ragbag. She was truly a sorry sight.

And Will couldn't take his eyes off of her.

Chapter Six

Emmeline was thankful that Johnny and some of the others had finally arrived in town and that she and her mother and sisters had found a warm, sheltered place in which to spend at least one night while her brother bunked with the single men.

The women from the wagon train, along with the female displaced residents, were being housed in the church basement, and the few men who had decided to catch forty winks were bunking on the main floor or outside in what was left of their covered wagons, now that the rain had ceased.

The slim, dark-haired, young local woman who had provided a kerosene lamp and a basin in which to wash had introduced herself to the group as Cassandra Garrison, Zeb's sister. As Cassandra bustled about the dimly lit basement room, Emmeline did her best to tend to Bess. It was hard to manage without adequate light.

"Excuse me, Miss Garrison, could you bring that lamp closer for a moment?" she asked as the young woman hurried past.

"Of course. I'm here to help."

"Thank you. Just hold it up so I can look after my sister's wounds, will you?"

"Wounds? Oh, dear, has the doctor seen her?"

"In a manner of speaking," Emmeline said, letting her ill will show. "He didn't seem to think a bump on the head was anything to be concerned about. He gave her laudanum and told me to put her to bed. I was not favorably impressed with his medical expertise."

"I know exactly what you mean." Cassandra sighed. "Have you met my brother, Zeb? He's been trying for ages to get a decent doctor to come to High Plains. So far, he's had no success."

"Anybody should be better than the one you have."

"Amen to that." She lowered her voice and eyed Bess as some of the nearby travelers began to snore. "Did she say what happened to her?"

"No. She hasn't spoken a word since the tornado. I'm worried."

"Little wonder," Cassandra said. "I'd be worried, too. How did you manage to get to town?"

"We hitched a ride with a friendly rancher."

"Oh, so that was you. I'd heard that Will Logan

had brought some folks in. Oh, dear, then it was your father who was…"

"Yes," Emmeline said, speaking aside and away from where her mother already slept. "Papa was killed."

"I'm so sorry. Zeb and I are the only Garrisons left, too. It's hard, but at least we have each other. And you have family, too. That must be comforting."

"It is. I'm just not sure how we're going to get by."

"Can you go back where you came from?"

"No." Emmeline shook her head as she finished bathing the cuts in Bess's hair and gently eased her down onto the pallet. Thankfully, the girl was almost asleep already, probably due to the sedative the doctor had administered. "Papa cut all our ties when he sold the farm in central Missouri and disposed of everything but a few of our possessions. We have the clothes on our backs plus whatever we can manage to salvage from the prairie tomorrow. Chances are, most of our things will never be recovered."

"I'm so sorry. I think you and I are about the same size. I can give you a nice dress," Cassandra said, patting Emmeline's hand.

Feeling suddenly guilty for considering material possessions rather than concentrating on the twins, Emmeline nevertheless said, "Thank you," before she explained her true concerns. "We were traveling with orphaned children, eight-year-old twins, who are still missing. Even if I could somehow return to Missouri, I'd never leave Missy and Mikey behind."

"Oh, my. Is that who the men are out looking for?"

"I assume so. Will—Mr. Logan—said he would keep searching for as long as was necessary."

"If Will Logan made that promise you can bank on it," Cassandra said. "He's my brother's best friend."

"Have you lived here long?"

"Long enough. Zeb sent for me and some of the others as soon as he and Will were ready. High Plains has only been in existence for about two years. Why?"

"I just thought, if you were familiar with this place, you might be able to tell me what I could do to earn enough money to support my family. Is there a school here?"

"Yes," Cassandra said, "but I'm the teacher."

"How about cooking? I noticed a boardinghouse. Do they need someone?"

She shook her head. "Sorry. No. Rebecca Gundersen is doing that and she's very good."

"Oh." Sighing, Emmeline had to admit how totally spent she was. Still, she managed a smile for the amiable young woman. "Well, thank you anyway. I suppose something will turn up. If you happen to think of suitable work for me, or for my thirteen-year-old brother, please let us know?"

"I will. And I'll fetch the dress for you before morning. Good night. God keep you all."

"Good night. Thank you for everything."

As Cassandra left with the lamp, Emmeline settled onto the pallet next to Bess and Glory. She couldn't help thinking once again of how dire their circumstances were. Fretting, she started to turn to God in prayer, then hesitated. It had been far easier to exercise her faith when life was simpler and her family intact. Even Papa's presence, as difficult as he could be, had been comforting. And now he was gone.

That fact whirled in her head like the prairie wind that had changed everything in the space of a few terrifying minutes. She squeezed her eyes closed, hoping to blot out the remembered sights and sounds of the storm. It was no use. The frightening scene continued to haunt her as if it were all happening again. Wind blew so hard it hurt her ears. Dirt and hail pelted her. She could remember her mother's screams and imagine the ox crushing her father. Her heart began to race, her whole body trembled and her mouth felt as dry as cotton.

"What else could I have done?" Emmeline whispered, knowing there was no easy answer. "Why did this have to happen to us?"

Tears slid silently onto the coarse woolen blanket folded beneath her. In the blink of an eye, the weight of the world had landed on her shoulders and she would have to find the strength to bear up under it.

In her deepest heart she knew that God still cared, that He would not have given her more than she could bear, yet a perverse part of her nature insisted that this all had to be a dreadful mistake. A nightmare. A passing fancy that would prove to be nothing more than a bad dream that would be gone in the morning.

She clasped her hands together as if in prayer and opened her eyes. Nothing had changed. She was still lying on a rough blanket in the basement of a church, and what was left of her family still lay beside her.

This was no dream. It was all too real. And the trials were just beginning.

Will was exhausted. He and others had scoured the prairie with lanterns and torches for the better part of the night with no results other than a wagonload of the pioneers' goods that they'd gathered up during the course of the search.

He supposed returning to High Plains with something was better than coming back empty handed, even though they had not found what they were really looking for. There had been no sign of the missing children. Not a trace.

He dreaded facing Emmeline Carter with that news. In his heart he had truly believed he'd be successful and now he was going to have to admit defeat—at least for the time being. He was not going to quit looking. As time passed, the children's chances of recovery lessened, yes, but that didn't mean a good outcome was impossible. His God was in charge, so anything could happen.

Instead of cheering him, however, that thought brought his friend Pete's late wife and baby to mind. They hadn't deserved to die so young, yet they had. No one had any guarantees of another day or even one more moment of life. Life was a divine gift and should be considered such. For man to assume he was in charge of his own destiny was the ultimate folly.

Still, that did not mean it wasn't prudent to do one's best at all times, Will argued sensibly. The good Lord had given him the brains and means with which to aid his fellow man and so he would, no matter what.

As he strode toward the church, he steeled himself for what he was about to do. Telling Emmeline that the children in her care were still un-accounted for was going to be one of the most difficult tasks he had ever faced.

Wagons had been assembled into a makeshift camp and crowds were gathered around open cooking fires in the churchyard. The aroma of food reminded him that he hadn't eaten for longer than he could remember. Keeping body and soul together had not seemed at all important in the midst of the storm and its aftermath, but now his stomach was complaining. Loudly.

So many folks were bustling around, Will had to shoulder his way through to navigate the throng.

When someone handed him a warm biscuit and a tin cup of hot coffee he accepted with a quick thank-you, realizing belatedly that his makeshift waitress was Zeb's sister.

Recognizing her, he paused and smiled. "Morning, Cassandra."

"Good morning, Will. How did your place fare?"

"Well, considering. The worst of the storm by-passed the house and outbuildings. How about here? Is everybody accounted for?"

"Pretty much. At least as far as I know. I've never seen such a mess. It's going to take everyone's best efforts to set things right again. And these poor travelers are in worse shape than we are. At least we have the church and each other to rely upon."

Will took a deep breath and released it as a sigh. "Yeah." As he spoke he was scanning the group of women in the background who were busy preparing and serving food.

"She helped with the cooking earlier but I think she's back in the church basement, tending to her kin, now," Cassandra said with a knowing smile.

"What?" His eyebrows arched.

"Emmeline Carter. That's who you're looking for, isn't it?"

"How did you…?"

The young woman grinned at him. "How did I know? The look on your face said it all. That, and the fact that Miss Emmeline and I had a nice chat last night after you'd gone back to look for those missing twins."

"I wish I'd found them," he replied soberly.

"I know you did your best." She pointed past his shoulder. "I see they're bringing in more damaged wagons. Pete's going to have plenty of work to keep himself and Edward Gundersen busy for a good long while."

"That's the truth."

"Oh, and speaking of the Gundersens, your new friend Emmeline was asking if I knew of a job for her. She suggested cooking for the boardinghouse but I told her Rebecca was already doing that."

"Um." Will sipped the hot, strong coffee to wash down his biscuit. "I imagine there's no room for a kitchen helper, either. Plus, she'd have to have a place to stay for herself and all her kin, so she'd take up most of their rooms. That would never work."

"I know."

Will pushed his hat farther back on his head and yawned. "What they need is a spread with plenty of space." A notion was tickling his subconscious, insisting on being recognized. "Like mine, maybe?"

"I thought you'd never figure that out," Cassandra said with a light laugh and broad grin. "You must really be tired for it to take you so long."

"Yeah, but what am I going to do with Hank?"

"Send him out with your other hands to tend the

cattle. This is a busy season on the range, anyway. He'll probably be delighted to be out of the kitchen and back in the saddle again."

"Suppose she doesn't want to work for me?"

Cassandra laughed louder. "Suppose you ask her?"

"I could do that."

"You certainly could. And when you do, tell her it was my idea, which it was. That should help her decide in your favor."

"You don't think she'd accept otherwise?"

"If you explain that her family can live at the ranch with her, that should quiet any misgivings. I can tell she's not the type of woman to agree to move in with a bunch of rowdy bachelors like you and those cowhands of yours."

"We're just hardworking men," Will countered. "Besides, I thought you were sort of interested in my cowhand Clint. Or have you decided that Percival Walker is more to your liking?" He made a face when he mentioned the lawyer's name.

"I'm not ready to settle down with either of them," Cassandra said. "I don't care if my brother does think turning twenty-two makes me an old maid."

Smiling, Will handed her the empty tin cup and touched the brim of his hat politely. "You'll always be like a little sister to me, Cassandra." He chuckled. "A troublesome one."

"Then you should be used to dealing with strong-willed women," she said. "And that's just as well because I think I see Emmeline. Isn't that her coming out of the church?"

Will whirled. His heart leaped. Someone must have given her a clean dress, because she looked lovely. She'd managed to smooth her tangled hair and was striding toward him so purposefully it was as if he were the only person present. He certainly had eyes only for her.

As she was crossing the distance between them, three large, unkempt men who looked like the brothers he'd first seen out at the wreck tried to intercept her. Will wondered if he was going to have to intercede, but Emmeline deftly sidestepped to avoid the young ruffians and hurried past them.

Will doffed his hat in greeting, scowling and looking past her. "Good morning. Were those men from your wagon train?"

"Yes. The Tullys wouldn't know how to act polite if their lives depended upon it." She touched his forearm and he felt an unaccustomed shiver. "Never mind them. What of the children? Did you find them?"

"I'm sorry," Will said, noting that she immediately withdrew her hand.

Her shoulders slumped. "Was there—was there any sign? Anything at all?"

"Not that we could see at night."

"Then I must go back and look in the daylight," Emmeline said. "Will you loan me a horse?"

"I'll do better than that. I'll escort you, if that's what you want."

He could tell she was hesitant, unlike the bold way she had acted in the immediate aftermath of the tornado. "You're not afraid to ride alone with me again, are you?"

"No. Of course not. It's just that I don't want to leave Bess and Glory with only my mother to look after them. She's been ill."

"What are you going to do? In the long run, I mean. You can continue to stay at the church temporarily, of course, but you should be thinking about the future for you and your family."

"I don't have any idea."

It troubled Will to see how his question had distressed her. Perhaps it would be wiser, kinder, to offer her the job on his ranch immediately.

"I see. I was going to wait to ask you this, but since we're discussing it, I was wondering if you— and your family, of course—would like to stay at the Circle-L for a while. Just till you get back on your feet."

"Absolutely not. We will not accept charity."

"No, no. Not charity. I need a good cook. The one I have is barely adequate. And Cassandra said you were asking about a job. It would mean cooking for me and four other men, plus your kin, but it would give you a roof over your head and a bit of money, plus board."

"That's not fair to you, Mr. Logan. There are already five of us and, Lord willing, there will soon be two more. How can I possibly do enough work to pay for all that?"

"You let me worry about the details. Will you accept? Cassandra said to tell you it was her idea."

"Was it?" She arched a thin brow and studied him so closely he felt his cheeks begin to warm.

"Yes, and no. Let's just say she led our conversation in a way that made me think of offering. Well?"

"I don't know. My mother isn't well and we wouldn't want to be a burden."

"Suppose you let me worry about the details? Maybe the good Lord brought us together the way He did just so I'd be in a position to help you."

Emmeline rolled her eyes. "Please. I'm having enough trouble believing God even cares after all this, let alone giving Him credit for providing a way out of our dilemma."

"Please? You'll be doing me a great favor if you accept." He could tell she was struggling with her decision and he waited, barely breathing, until she finally nodded.

"All right. Hopefully, it will just be for a few days. I won't impose on your hospitality."

"Fine. I'll tell Pete to let me know as soon as your wagon is repaired and we can bring it out to the ranch, too. In the meantime, we recovered lots of lost belongings from the prairie last night." He pointed. "They're over there in that wagon. The first thing you and your family should do is reclaim your personal possessions before someone else takes them."

"What about going looking for the twins?"

"There's a fresh search party already doing that. If they don't succeed I'll loan you a horse and we can go together, later."

He saw her blue eyes grow misty. "I—we—don't know how to thank you, Mr. Logan."

"You can begin by calling me Will," he suggested. "Mr. Logan always reminds me of my father."

"That would not be appropriate," Emmeline said, dropping her gaze to study the ground at her feet. "If I am to be in your employ you may call me Emmeline, but I should not be so familiar with you. It's not seemly."

"Then at least make it Mr. Will and drop the Logan. It will please me more."

"Yes, sir."

Will could tell she had slipped into a subservient position and he didn't like that one bit. However, he wasn't going to argue. They did hardly know each other. Perhaps there would be time in the near future to develop the kind of casual camaraderie he had with Cassandra and a few others.

In a way, Emmeline was behaving wisely, he reasoned. Some of the local women were terrible gossips and prone to think the worst of their peers, especially pretty young ladies like Miss Carter. If her mother and siblings had not been moving out to the Circle-L with her, there was no telling how many rumors her presence there would cause.

And that was not only unfair, it would be bad for her in the future. If she remained in High Plains, keeping her good name would be crucial, especially in regard to her eventually finding a husband and making a new life for herself.

That thought hit Will like a punch in the stomach. There was nothing wrong with his logic. Most young women chose to marry and raise families and there were far more single men in and around High Plains than there were eligible women. A good marriage could be just the thing to salvage her family.

It was the idea of Emmeline Carter as someone else's bride that stuck in his craw.

Chapter Seven

The trip from High Plains to the Circle-L seemed to be taking forever. Emmeline was feeling the physical aftereffects of her tumble on the prairie, especially while riding in the spring wagon. She did her best to hide the pain that shot up her spine with every jolt of the stiff springs, but the discomfort was keeping her from fully enjoying the balmy weather, clear blue skies and drifts of wildflowers that bordered the narrow trail.

Her mother had offered little comment about their temporary living arrangements and Bess was still mute, so the only objections Emmeline had had to deal with were from Johnny and Glory.

The five-year-old was merely impatient to arrive at their destination and be let out of the wagon. Johnny, on the other hand, had resisted her authority and had immediately started cursing when she'd told him of her plans for the family. He had continued to express himself that way until Will had taken him aside and had a brief talk with him.

Emmeline couldn't hear everything the man was saying. She did hear him tell her brother that he was lucky to have a grown-up sister who was so smart and capable, and that he should show her proper respect.

Instead of agreeing, Johnny began to pout. That was typical of him. However, as long as the boy had settled down and was behaving himself, Emmeline figured she'd tolerate his regrettable attitude and let him sulk. In his case, silence was a blessing.

Across her lap she held the one possession she'd never expected to see again: her dulcimer. It was a fragile, four-stringed instrument, hourglass shaped, and had been found lying beside the trail, astonishingly unharmed. When she'd spied it among the salvaged items Will had brought back to town she'd nearly wept for joy. The plaintive sound of its music was perfect for hymns or ballads or just random, soothing strumming. That dulcimer had eased her emotions often and, now that she had it back, she knew it would do so again. Except for the missing children, there was nothing Will Logan could have given her that would have blessed her heart more.

The others were settled in the bed of the wagon, comfortably surrounded by clothing, bedding and sundry other salvaged belongings. Emmeline rode on the driver's seat beside Will. The sun was already high before they reached a rise from which he could stop the team and point out his ranch.

"There it is," he said proudly.

She was taken aback. Instead of the large home and array of outbuildings she had envisioned, there seemed to be little there. The main house was a simple, rectangular structure that looked as if it consisted of no more than two or three rooms. The barn was the largest and most impressive building. Beyond that was a partially constructed, narrow dwelling that she suspected housed the ranch hands.

"It's—nice," she managed to say.

"It's coming along. I just ordered more lumber to expand the bunkhouse, but I suppose that will have to wait till Zeb takes care of the places in town that were damaged. Those folks need it worse than I do right now."

"Is there room for all of us?"

"We'll make room," Will said pleasantly. "Your brother and I can bunk with the cowhands and you women can have my room."

"Absolutely not."

He arched an eyebrow and nodded toward the back of the wagon where her mother and sisters rode. "Would you have me put them in the bunk-house, instead?"

"No, but—"

"Then we'll have no arguments. You should be

nearest the kitchen, and the rest of your family needs to be with you. Your brother's nearly a man. It won't hurt him to start acting like one. And, when your mama and sister get to feeling better, they can help you, too."

"Of course," Emmeline said, refusing to voice the thoughts that followed. It had been years since Mama had made much effort to care for the family. She'd lain in a sickbed more often than not. And Bess, who had usually been the most help, was just sitting there and blankly staring into the distance. If there was housework to be done besides the cooking, Emmeline figured she was going to have to do most of it herself.

She sat up straighter, raised her chin and accepted her fate. She would do this. And without help if need be. She had wanted a place to live and a decent job that would support her family and now she had one. If she had to continue to labor alone, so be it. She would be grateful. She *was* grateful. Beyond that, she would simply take one day at a time and deal with its problems and trials as they arose.

Shading her eyes with her hand and peering at the ranch that lay below, she began to see how its owner might be proud of it no matter how primitive it was. He had come to the high plains and begun to build a life for himself. Where there had been nothing, he now had a home, a future, a chance to succeed.

It gave her something to aspire to, for herself and her family.

* * *

Since Will had already swung by to check the welfare of his house and barn and found them solid, he felt comfortable inviting the Carter family to move in with him. It wasn't the state of the buildings that really worried him anyway. It was the attitudes of the men. His ranch hands had no say in his decisions, of course, but he wasn't keen on breaking the news to old Hank that his place in the kitchen had just been usurped. And by a pretty young woman, to boot.

Dogs were circling the wagon and barking a welcome when Will drove between the rear of the house and the barn. Chickens squawked and scattered. Horses in a corral trotted up to the rail fence to look with curiosity upon the strange rig and whinny to the team. Graceful, orange-breasted swallows soared in and out of the hayloft above the main barn door.

Hank was wiping his hands on a dirty apron and scowling when he came out of the house and greeted them in the muddy yard. "We wondered when you was comin' home, Will. What took ya so long? Did ya buy a new team and wagon?"

"Nope. I borrowed this rig so I wouldn't have to come home to get a wagon. I'd have been here sooner but I was busy leading a search party," he said, climbing down and reaching back to assist Emmeline so she could disembark without her clean dress touching the mud-coated wheel rims. "There were some children missing. Still are."

"Too bad." The older man's bushy gray eyebrows knit above steely blue eyes. "Did ya take in the whole wagon train?"

Will laughed. "Only part of it." He helped the others out of the wagon bed and started to introduce them, beginning with Joanna. "This is Mrs. Carter and these are her children. Their wagon is at Pete's for repairs, so they'll be staying here for a while."

"You serious?"

"Very." He lightly cupped Emmeline's elbow and urged her to step forward. "This is the oldest daughter. She's going to be cooking for us. I need you more on the range, Hank. Always have. I just didn't know of anybody else who could keep us well fed."

The crusty old man's reaction was worse than Will had imagined. He spat into the dirt and glared as if he'd just been fired. Whipping off the apron, he wadded it into a ball, threw it aside and stalked off without another intelligible word, although Will read plenty in the movement of his lips as he passed.

Will shrugged, then turned to Emmeline and smiled. "That went well, don't you think?"

She rolled her eyes at him. "Oh, yes. Definitely. He was delighted to be relieved of kitchen chores."

"I thought so." Will gave a cynical chuckle. "Hank never was a man of many words and in this case, it's probably just as well. Your brother might have learned some bad ones he didn't already know."

"I doubt that," she said. "My father's language used to be quite colorful." Pausing, she asked, "Are you certain you want to go through with this? I mean, given the attitude of that man and what the rest are likely to think, perhaps it's best that we don't stay."

"Nonsense. This is my spread. They work for me. Whatever I say, goes. And I say you stay, for as long as you want the job."

"All right."

She shooed the curious ranch dogs away as she reached for the dirty apron, lifted it from the puddle where it had landed and held it out between thumb and forefinger to watch it drip. "I think the first thing to do is thoroughly scrub that kitchen. I'll also need to know what you want for supper and when to have it ready."

"I'll show you folks the springhouse and the other facilities, too. Then we can move your things into the bedroom and take my stuff out."

"I still don't think—"

"Like I said, everybody works for me, including you, so you have to do it my way."

"Are you always this stubborn?"

"Only when I know I'm right, which is pretty much all the time."

When Emmeline smiled and said, "That's what

I thought," before starting for the house, he had to laugh. If old Hank thought his tantrum was going to deter or frighten her, he had another think coming. This woman had coped with a cruel father and goodness knows what else all her life. A grumpy ranch hand was not going to scare her off. Not in a million years.

And besides, Will thought as his stomach rumbled, her cooking *had* to be better than Hank's. The old man's biscuits were always hard enough to bust a tooth and his coffee was so strong it practically dissolved the bowl of a spoon. If Emmeline Carter was even half the cook that Rebecca Gundersen was, she was going to be the best addition to the ranch that he'd ever made.

Emmeline hadn't been surprised to find few amenities in the spacious but primitive kitchen. The sink was small and she knew she'd dearly miss having a Hoosier cabinet available for easy baking preparation. The plain, plank kitchen table would suffice, however, once she'd scrubbed it a lot cleaner than its former caretaker had, and it was nice to be back in a real kitchen after all the effort it took to prepare a decent meal within the wagon train.

It was going to be better having a real, iron cookstove than trying to keep an open fire burning properly, too, even if the stove's edges had looked as if they were coated with enough grease to make soap.

And using wood for fuel instead of buffalo chips was going to be a definite improvement. Splitting and fetching wood was one of the chores she intended to assign to her brother in the days to come. Johnny could also fetch water for the house. With several springs close by, he wouldn't even have to draw it from a well.

Emmeline had finally finished scrubbing and begun cooking. She was standing beside the rustic table, cutting lard into the center of an enormous bowl of flour, when she sensed someone at her elbow. It was Bess!

Emmeline's heart swelled with hope and anticipation at her sister's arrival. This was the first time since the twister that Bess had moved a step without being guided or prodded. To have her appear in the kitchen so suddenly was definitely a good sign, though her visage was a far cry from the lively, eager girl Bess had been before the accident.

As Emmeline studied her sister she realized that there wasn't the spark of understanding in her expression that she'd come to expect. Nevertheless, she smiled broadly and stepped aside to make room.

"I was hoping you'd come to help. I've just started the biscuits."

The girl didn't answer, but she did reach for a pitcher of milk and pour a little into the depression in the flour.

Emmeline continued to work, kneading and

mixing with her hands. "I found some pearlash for this and I'll set a sponge tonight for baking bread tomorrow. It's truly amazing how few of the usual necessities are here." She paused and smiled at her sister again. "Do you want to help? You can finish these biscuits for me if you'd like. We don't seem to have a cutter, but I did find an old, round tin that I think will do fine."

Bess took Emmeline's place at the table and rolled the sleeves of her dress up to her elbows, but remained silent.

It wasn't the enormous step forward that Emmeline had hoped for, but at least the girl was beginning to take notice of normal daily life. That had to be good.

Another good thing was the pleasant, welcoming aroma of the stew and the spotless kitchen. How anyone had put up with the kind of so-called housekeeping that Hank had done was beyond comprehension. It was going to take her a week or better to catch up with just the most basic chores he had ignored and to put things right. She was determined to prove her worth—to him and to all the others.

It was a blessing to be able to use her talents for the support of her family, and she was going to do over and above the basics until she had astounded her boss and his men with her prowess in the kitchen.

That thought made her smile. Will Logan seemed easy to please, yet she knew she had to establish herself in the ranch's staff by her skill. Those other men were surely not going to welcome her with open arms, especially if they sided with Hank about losing his cook's job.

And, chances were, the old man would get his position back before long, Emmeline mused. She wasn't planning to stay long at the Circle-L. But while she was there, she was going to go all-out.

There were no screens on the small windows and the kitchen was getting so hot that Emmeline propped open the door, sorry at once when insects began to congregate.

"Glory, get in here and help us," she called. "I need you to fan the table."

As the little blond girl skipped into the kitchen, Emmeline was touched by how happy and carefree she seemed. Had *she* ever been filled with childish joy like that? She doubted it. For as far back as she could recall, she had fretted about her siblings and Mama, going out of her way to protect them.

And that same concern had extended to Missy and Mikey from the moment her family had taken them in, she remembered. Their young parents had been neighbors of the Carters, back in Missouri. Their mama had taken sick first, then their papa. The fever had come and gone in mere days, sparing the children but leaving them orphans. And because the two families had grown so close, Joanna Carter had insisted they bring the twins into their home. It was one of the only times in Emmeline's memory when her mother had stood her ground and insisted on getting her way, although in the long run, Papa had won. He had agreed to take the twins with them on the trail only if they were eventually placed with another couple, either along the way or once they arrived in Oregon.

Perhaps, after the evening meal, she and Will could ride out onto the prairie again and add their eyes to those of the other searchers. Surely someone would find something soon. Anything. Even the worst news had to be better than not knowing what fate had befallen those lost babes.

Will pushed back from the supper table, fully sated. He didn't know about the other men, but he couldn't recall ever having eaten a better-tasting meal. It was far from fancy, yet as good as the finest in all of Massachusetts. The only thing missing was dessert, and Emmeline had promised to bake apple pies as soon as he got her some dried fruit to stew up for the filling. He'd gladly ride all the way to Manhattan or Council Grove if Johnson's didn't have any. It had been ages since he'd actually looked forward to eating at the ranch and he was going to do all he could to support her efforts.

Pale, Joanna Carter and her three daughters cleared the table while most of the men retired outside to relax and roll smokes.

Only Will tarried to speak with Emmeline. "That was delicious."

"Thank you." She smiled. "I thought everyone was pleased. Except maybe Hank."

"He's just jealous. He dumped so much salt on his plate it's a wonder he was able to choke the food down."

"I noticed." Her smile faded. "I know it's getting late, but I thought maybe we could make a quick trip out to where we lost the twins. I think there's a full moon tonight."

"There is. And no cloud cover to speak of." He nodded toward the others and lowered his voice. "Are you sure your mother and Bess can handle this?"

"I'll lend a hand before we leave. Mama looks better than she has in ages, and Bess helped me prepare supper so they should be able to handle drying and putting away the dishes. Just give me time to do that and grab a coat. Mine is still water-logged but Papa's will work."

When she had finished her chores, Will followed her into the front of the house and watched as she donned the oversize coat. "What about your brother? Does he ride?"

"Of course. Why?"

"Because I worry about your reputation. If he goes with us there should be no question of improprieties."

"I see. All right. But I assure you, I'm not worried. I've already told you that I trust you."

"I'm flattered." Will gestured toward the open door with his hat. "Come on. Let's go saddle some horses and make tracks."

When they reached the yard, Will noted that the oldest man and the boy were not with the others. He questioned Clint. "Where's Hank?"

"Beats me. He went round back of the barn."

"Johnny, too?"

The lanky cowboy shrugged. "Reckon so."

Emmeline's eyes widened as her gaze darted to Will. "Uh-oh."

"Yeah. It doesn't sound good, does it?" Stepping out, he started across the still-damp ground. She had to hike up her long skirts, dodge puddles and take two steps for every one of his strides to keep pace.

They rounded the corner of the barn together and stopped abruptly. Hank had obviously been sharing homemade smokes with the boy. Judging by the retching Johnny was doing, the experience had not agreed with him.

Will glared at the older man as he grabbed the boy by the collar and dragged him back toward the bunk-house. "You sleep in here tonight. And see that you don't go to bed until your stomach has settled or I'll have you mopping the place all night, you hear?"

The miserable thirteen-year-old merely nodded.

Keeping her distance, Emmeline sighed. "Well, there sits our chaperone. What shall we do now?"

"I say we go anyway," Will answered. "Unless you're worried about your reputation."

"I'm a lot more worried about those lost children," she said flatly. "Every night they spend on the prairie is going to be harder. I keep picturing them, cold and hungry and waiting for someone like us to rescue them."

He couldn't see her expression very well in the twilight, but he could hear the pathos in her voice. If there had been some way, any way, to guarantee success he'd have implemented it.

In reality, all he could do, all anyone could do, was keep looking. And keep praying.

Chapter Eight

Prairie darkness seemed to close in around Emmeline like an invisible shroud, and the farther they rode from the ranch, the worse it got. She had never before feared anything about the night except that threat that her own father had brought by his mere presence. Many a time she had lain in bed, quaking, as she'd listened to him rant and throw things while railing at her mother about the most insignificant trifles, but nothing else had frightened her, not even the nights they'd spent practically in the wild with the wagon train.

Now, leaving the comfort of the house, of her family, she was seized by an unfamiliar sense of foreboding, of dread. The only thing that kept her from reining in her horse hard and heading back from whence they'd come was the steadying, dependable presence of Will Logan riding beside her.

As her eyes adjusted to the moonlight, she began to see more details. That was, unfortunately, far from reassuring. Amongst the grasses she imagined animal shapes, human shapes, lurking and ready to pounce. And atop the black outline of the hills she saw more than cottonwoods. She saw mounted Indians. At least she thought she did. One moment they would be there and the next they'd be gone.

When Will asked, "Are you all right?" she decided to tell him the unvarnished truth.

"No. I'm not," Emmeline said. "I know I should be concentrating on looking for the twins, but I keep imagining danger lurking, instead."

"You mean the Indians?"

She caught her breath. "You saw them, too? They're really there?"

"Yes."

"Oh, dear. I was already nervous when I thought it was all in my head. Now I'm good and scared."

"There's no need to worry," Will said calmly. "I know some of them, and the others shouldn't be much of a problem as long as we're well armed and keep our distance."

"Speak for yourself," she countered. "I didn't bring Papa's rifle. I don't even know what happened to it after the storm."

"I suppose it'll turn up, providing the Indians didn't scavenge it before the searchers from town had a chance to pick it up for you. I didn't notice any guns among the things we hauled back to town."

"Nor did I."

Will patted the scabbard attached to his saddle. "Don't fret about it. I brought a rifle besides my revolver. We'll be fine."

"I'd still feel better if I were armed, too," she said.

"Since you're so accomplished at everything else, I assume you can shoot straight?"

"Oh, yes. I taught Johnny to hunt rabbits with a little squirrel gun, back home in Missouri. I suppose that gun's gone for good, too." She sighed. "So much has changed in such a short time it's hard for me to take it all in."

"Possessions can be replaced," Will said. "It's the people who are most important—and you still have your mother and sisters."

She detected slight amusement in his tone when he belatedly added, "And Johnny."

"My brother used to be a good boy. Then, as he got older, he began to act more and more like Papa. I caught him torturing one of our barn cats not long before we left home. I made him stop, but when I told Papa he just laughed as if he was proud that his son was acting so cruel."

"I'm sure there were some good things about your father," Will said. "Why don't you try to concentrate on those?"

"It's not easy."

"I know. My father was the same kind of man. He was the reason I left home when I was not much older than your brother is now."

"Is your father still living?" she asked.

Will's voice was low when he answered, and Emmeline could tell he was moved. "No. He and my mother both perished a few years ago."

Refraining from further discussion, she rode along beside him while her thoughts spun. She and Will Logan did have a little in common because of their fathers. However, that was where their similarities ended. He was an established rancher with land and a bright future, while she had an uncertain future at best, especially while she had the weight of her whole family on her shoulders.

That, and the fate of Missy and Mikey, she added, further chagrined. Will was right about the need to control and direct her thoughts. If she permitted her imagination free rein, it took her into the depths of despair. That was wrong. And foolish. They had a job to do and woolgathering was counterproductive.

"How much farther?" she asked when he reined in atop a low rise.

"Just down there is where your wagon ended up." He pointed. "It was near that grove of cottonwoods with their tops broken off. Can you see the spot?"

"Yes. I think so. Thank the Lord we have plenty of moonlight tonight."

"Right. As long as the clouds stay at bay we'll

be able to see fairly well." He stretched and the saddle leather creaked. "You ready?"

"As ready as I'll ever be," Emmeline replied. "Lead on."

Part of her wanted to stop, to return to the ranch and its comfort, its safety, yet she knew her duty lay below. And so, probably, did the Indian scavengers. If she could see the shadowy, broken trees and perhaps other refuse from the original incident, then it stood to reason that the Kansa could also see her approaching.

That notion sent a shiver up her spine the likes of which she had experienced when first spying her father's crushed body.

She gave her horse a nudge so it wouldn't lag behind. The sooner they covered the nearby prairie and called it a night, the sooner her heart would quit racing and her palms stop perspiring.

To say she was frightened was like saying the killer tornado had been nothing but a zephyr.

Will had little hope they'd find the missing children after the other fruitless searches, but for Emmeline's sake he vowed to keep trying. There would come a time when even she would give up and admit defeat, he was sure, but as long as she still wanted to keep looking he'd oblige her.

They rode down to the rutted wagon trail, then paused. There was little left to mark the site of the

Carter wreck except a few splintered boards and some scraps of canvas. Someone, probably hungry Indians, had dragged off the ox carcass and butchered it after Amos Carter's body had been moved to town for burial. Coyotes had quickly disposed of the rest of the animal, leaving almost no sign of the recent tragedy other than a skull and backbone.

Will waited for Emmeline to stop her horse next to his before he spoke. "We searched to the north and east pretty thoroughly yesterday and last night. Do you want to try going west this time?"

"Do you think they could have been carried backward because the twister was spinning?"

"Honestly? I doubt it. The whole storm moved east."

"Then we'll go over the same ground again in the hopes that the others missed something. I don't have a very good sense of direction, especially out here with no big landmarks, so you'll have to take the lead."

"Okay." He gently nudged the sorrel's flanks with his heels and started into the tall grass. "Follow me."

Will trusted the horses to stay together even if Emmeline wasn't paying close enough attention. That allowed him to concentrate on the areas to both sides of the trail that their passage was cutting through the bluestem. Most of that prairie grass was already as high as the horse's chests and beyond, making their quest nearly impossible. Still, he pressed on, calling the twins' names frequently.

The farther Will and Emmeline traveled from the marked trail, the more edgy he became. It must have been the suggestion of fear that the young woman had placed in his mind that was making him feel jumpy, he reasoned, fighting growing anxiety. He'd been on the plains alone at night many times, yet had never felt quite this uneasy, not even when groups of Kansa Indians were clearly close by.

Scanning the distant rise for signs of them and noting nothing unusual, he concluded that he was unduly anxious because he now had Emmeline's well-being to worry about as well as his own. Sure. That was it. He was just a bit more nervous than usual because she was with him.

In addition, there was his lingering fear that if they did locate them, the children would no longer be alive. That unacceptable yet likely notion gave him the chills. Of all the things he had imagined and dreaded, that was by far the worst scenario.

And, now that they had traveled so far afield, he was getting ready to suggest that they give up for the present and return to the ranch. He knew Emmeline would object. He also knew that she had to be exhausted from her recent ordeal.

Halting his sorrel, Will stood in the stirrups and swiveled to address Emmeline. He opened his mouth to speak and gasped, instead.

He was alone. There was no sign of her.

* * *

The disturbance in the grass to one side of the raw trail was slight, yet it caught Emmeline's attention. Without thinking, she slowed her mount slightly and leaned over to study it more closely.

Something drew her, kept her interest in spite of a lack of concrete evidence. The path of broken grass was small—and while she had little tracking experience, it seemed too narrow to have belonged to any of the search party that had gone through this area earlier. It could have been caused by an animal, but…was she fooling herself to think the size seemed right for a child? Perhaps. And perhaps her eyes were simply sharper than those of previous searchers and had caught something they had all missed.

There was no doubt that she cared more for the twins than the others did because she knew and loved them both. The poor little things would have had no one if she and her mother hadn't intervened and rescued them. If it hadn't been for Amos…

"No." Emmeline stopped herself short. Will was right about the need to control her thoughts and she would, as much as was humanly possible. Yes, her father had been the reason the twins were not adopted by her own family, but he had allowed Mama to bring them along on the trip. In retrospect, an idea that had seemed best at the time was now not wise in the least. But how was anyone to know there would be a tornado? And how could they have anticipated the storm's terrible outcome?

Keeping hold of the reins, Emmeline swung her right leg over the saddle and kicked loose with her left foot to slide easily to the damp ground. She knew she might have difficulty remounting the tall gelding without help, but that was an insignificant concern at present. Although she couldn't make out any tracks in the mud, she could tell that its surface had been disturbed. The grass here was bent and broken, too, as if someone or something had recently passed through it. Maybe the searchers hadn't overlooked the path after all. Maybe it was new, created in the past few hours from Missy and Mikey heading in this direction.

Her heart leaped, expectant and cautiously joyful. That might be a good sign. If the children had wandered around in this tall vegetation, that meant they were still all right, not too injured to move or respond if she called to them.

She spoke their names softly at first. "Missy? Mikey? Are you there? It's me, Emmeline."

No answer came. She stepped forward with caution, choosing her path carefully, slowly, as she sought to avoid the boggier areas. "Missy? Answer me. Please?"

Although she kept talking, she refrained from shouting for fear Indians might overhear. They were still out there. They had to be. She could feel their

presence the same way a wild animal sensed the
approach of a hunter.

That thought made her shiver in spite of the
warmth provided by her father's old coat. The
garment was too big for her, but she'd chosen to
wear it because her own wraps were still damp.
And because Mama had always insisted that she
dress warmly against the night chill.

Now, Emmeline was sorry to be burdened by the
heavy garment. Its hem kept catching on the stubble
at her feet and hindered her passage even more than
her skirt and petticoats.

Working her way farther and farther off the trail
in pursuit of whoever or whatever had broken down
the grass stalks, she began to feel decidedly nervous.

The long coat snagged on a heavy tree limb that
she assumed had been snapped off by the twister.
Many of the cottonwoods she'd seen had been badly
battered, both on the prairie and back in High Plains,
leaving massive, troublesome refuse like this behind.

When repeated tugging failed to free her, she
braced herself and gave the coat a hard yank.

It came loose from the snag with a rip. One side
flipped into the air like the wings of a giant bird.

Startled, the horse reared and pulled the reins
from her grasp.

Emmeline screamed instinctively, afraid the descending hooves were going to strike her before
she could jump out of the way.

That was too much for the otherwise docile animal. It snorted, wheeled and galloped back the way they'd come, its tail held high in alarm.

She was thunderstruck. Breathless. Flabbergasted. What had she done?

Eyes wide, she looked right and left, then turned in a circle to try to get her bearings. She suddenly became aware of how foolish she'd been to wander off without Will. But surely, Will wasn't that far away and would soon appear, ready to chastise her for going off alone.

But he didn't. There was no sign of anyone or anything other than her. She held her breath and listened. A whip-poor-will called in the distance. Another answered. A coyote howled, joined immediately by other members of its pack. There had been a time when Emmeline had likened their calls to singing. Not this time. Now, they sounded as if they were preparing to encircle and devour her!

She clasped her hands and closed her eyes, intending to pray. No words came. Nor was there the peace and assurance she had hoped for.

Opening her eyes, she glanced down. What was that? It looked like a narrow piece of cloth stuck halfway up a stalk of the wiry grass.

Hand trembling, she reached for it. Touched it. Could barely believe what she'd found. It was a pink ribbon! The same kind that Missy had been wearing in her hair when she'd disappeared.

Emmeline cupped her hand around her mouth and shouted, "Missy! Mikey! Over here."

There was a rustling in the grass nearby. A figure began to rise.

In an instant, Emmeline realized that she was not about to be reunited with the twins.

Instead, she was looking straight into the darkly menacing face of an Indian.

Will had just started to retrace his path when he heard a woman scream. *Emmeline!* It had to be her.

He reined in his horse with a loud "Whoa," and listened, hoping, praying there would be another outburst so he could get a better idea of where the sound had originated.

Silence enveloped him. Beyond the heavy breathing of his horse—and himself—there was no other noise. Then he heard hooves pounding and a distant horse's whinny.

His sorrel answered the call. Will's heart leaped. That was exactly what he'd counted on when he'd permitted Emmeline to follow him instead of insisting she ride abreast. Like all horses, these two stablemates wanted to be together and would soon reunite their riders.

He relaxed as the horse approached, ready to greet Emmeline gladly, yet preparing to lecture her on the folly of letting herself fall behind.

The tall grasses parted. The lathered horse

skidded to a stop, flanks muddy and stirrup leathers flapping.

Will's heart pounded as he leaned to grab the loose reins. There was no rider to reprimand. The saddle was empty. Emmeline was gone.

In an instant he decided what to do. Leading her mount, he followed the trail it had left as it crashed through the grasses. They were pliable, yes, but the passage of an animal as large as that horse had left enough temporary damage to point the way.

He knew that in a short time there would be no trail to follow because the prairie would recover, as it always did. He had to hurry while he could still tell which way to go.

A cloud scudded across the full moon, temporarily dimming its light.

"No," Will muttered. "Please, God, no. Not now. I need to see."

As if in answer, the cloud passed on, although Will could tell at a glance that others were gathering and might soon blot out the moonlight altogether.

There had been a lantern hung on the front of Emmeline's saddle, but he could see that it was no longer there, meaning either she had removed it or the horse had thrown it off during its wild dash.

Will didn't care which it was. Nor did he have time to waste looking for a branch with which to fashion a torch. Some of the vegetation was already starting to spring back into place. Before long, there would be little clear sign left to follow, especially in the dark. And then what would happen to Emmeline? She had trusted him to look after her and he had failed.

It did occur to him that, unless she'd been thrown, she had probably had a hand in her own disappearance. But that was a moot point. She was gone. Alone on the open prairie and probably scared to death.

And it was all his fault.

Chapter Nine

The looming figure froze, his visage barely more than a black shadow as a cloud covered the moon, blocking the light.

Emmeline would have screamed in fear if she'd been able to make any sound at all. She opened her mouth. Nothing came out. Not even a squawk. She wanted to pray, to call out to God, but her mind could find no words.

The Indian's grin was a leer. He reached for her. Grabbed her arm. Twisted it.

She put her palms against his chest to push him away and felt bare flesh! Acting on instinct and raw fear, she threw herself backward and jerked free. As she pulled away, her hand closed over a necklace the man wore and she felt it break, scattering beads like a rain of pebbles.

Emmeline took a faltering step. Her heel caught

on the broken limb that had been at the heart of the whole incident. Arms cartwheeling, she fought to stay on her feet. It was no use. She was falling. Helpless. Vulnerable.

She hit the ground with a jolt that aggravated her prior injuries enough to send shock waves up her spine and finally force a noise from her. Instead of the usual embarrassed gasp and quick recovery that such an accident might engender, she let loose with a scream that was so loud, so long, it rang across the otherwise silent prairie and echoed back upon itself in a harmony of terror.

That was enough to loosen all of Emmeline's inhibitions. She drew another deep breath and repeated her scream, all the while staring at the figure of the Indian.

Other than his white teeth, she couldn't see his expression in detail, but she did see him brace himself and raise his arms in self-defense as if expecting an attack.

Again and again she continued to scream, each one more high-pitched and panicky than those previous. Her throat hurt. She could barely catch her breath. Yet she continued to shriek.

It seemed as if minutes passed, though she knew it had been mere seconds since she and the Indian had come face-to-face. He stepped back. His head swiveled furtively from side to side.

She managed a word within her screeching and stretched it out until her breath failed her. "Wi-i-i-il!"

The shadowy figure spun and ducked into the long grasses to disappear! She blinked, hardly able to believe what had just occurred. She was alone, unarmed and helpless, yet her adversary was the one who was running away! *Praise God.* She had not been able to pray properly, the way she'd been taught all her life, yet the Lord had known her need and had answered her wordless plea for deliverance.

Recovering her wits, she thought she heard the pounding of horse's hooves. Was the Indian riding off? Had he summoned help? *No.* The sound was coming from the other direction. From the way she assumed she had come.

Emmeline gathered her skirts and struggled to her feet just in time to see a horseman approaching at full gallop.

From the moment she spied him, she had no doubt who it was. She'd have recognized Will Logan under any circumstances and he was certainly a more than welcome sight.

He dismounted at a run, the same way she'd seen cowboys do when they were roping range cattle, and started toward her, wielding his rifle.

Emmeline had never been so glad to greet anyone in her entire life. Forgetting everything else, she flung herself into his arms and clung to him the way a drowning mariner might grip a floating piece of flotsam.

He pulled her close in spite of the long gun in his right hand. "What happened?"

"It's all over now. He's gone."

"Who? Who's gone?"

"An Indian. He ran away."

Will drew her to one side and stood ready to fire if necessary. "What makes you so sure?"

"I saw him leave. He was really in a hurry after I started to scream." Loath to let go, she continued to embrace her rescuer and felt him trembling along with her. That was both surprising and unnerving. If Will Logan believed there was that much danger, then perhaps she was not overreacting, either.

"What did he look like?"

"I—I don't know. It was dark. But I'm sure he was Indian." She recalled the warm feel of her attacker's bare chest and felt woozy. "There was something strange about his head. I could only see a shadowy outline, but his hair seemed to be all in the middle, like a horse's roached mane. It stood up oddly. Do you think he was wearing feathers?"

"I doubt it. The Kansa warriors pluck their faces and most of their scalp, except for a section in the center," Will said. "That's probably what made him look different." He gave her a squeeze. "I can't believe he didn't make off with you."

She shivered, still needing his proximity and unwilling to step away, though she knew she was acting improperly. Never in her memory had she willingly remained this close to any grown man, not even her own father, and she was amazed at how safe and cared for she felt.

She could sense Will's heart racing, as was hers, and could almost imagine that his warm breath was ruffling her hair, now that her bonnet was hanging behind her by its strings.

"We should be getting back to the ranch," he finally said. "Are you going to be able to ride?"

"Of course. But my horse…"

"I have him. He's the reason I was able to locate you so quickly. I followed his trail."

"Wait!" Emmeline suddenly stepped back and scanned the ground at their feet. "I have to show you something. I hope I haven't lost it in all the confusion. No. There it is."

Bending, she picked up the scraggly pink ribbon and held it for Will to see. "Look. I'm sure this is Missy's."

"There must be lots of stuff like that all over out here since the storm. Are you sure it's hers?"

Sobering, she nodded. "Fairly certain. I'll be positive when I've looked at it in the daylight and shown it to Bess and Mama."

"What else is down here?" he asked, crouching to pick up some shiny metal objects that caught his eye.

"I—I guess that's part of the Indian's necklace,"

Emmeline said, once again momentarily unsteady. "I had forgotten. It broke while we were struggling."

"That settles it. He was Kansa. They wear strings of shiny tin trinkets, like buttons, or sometimes bear claws, for decoration." He paused and tensed, scanning the dark prairie and dropping the buttons at his feet. "He'll be back for those. Mount up. It's time we hightailed it home."

"But…what about the hair ribbon? Suppose Missy and Mikey are close by? Shouldn't we look a little longer?"

"Not assuming your Indian friend is planning to go get reinforcements. I can only hold off a few at a time with this rifle. If they get close enough for me to shoot with a pistol, they're too close for comfort."

"I can't just leave those helpless children."

"You need to accept that the twins are probably beyond help," he said flatly, his tone tearing at Emmeline's heart. "Chances are, that ribbon was lost during the original storm, not tonight. If its owner is still anywhere nearby, it's because the Indians have already gotten to her and carried her off."

"Don't say that!"

"Somebody has to," Will argued. "You can't help the children by staying. You can only put yourself at greater risk. So either you come with me right now, of your own free will, or I'll sling you over the saddle and haul you home like a sack of potatoes."

"You wouldn't."

"Try me."

"Will they hurt the children?" Emmeline asked more quietly, fighting tears as she reluctantly accepted his ultimatum.

"No. Healthy ones are either adopted or put to work as slaves. They're valuable, just like a good horse." He made a step with his hands to assist her in mounting.

Emmeline swung aboard, took up the reins and slipped her feet into the stirrups before she asked, "Would they have done that with Bess, too?"

When Will answered, "No. She would probably have been made a wife," it didn't really shock her.

"That's what he would have done to me, too, isn't it?" Emmeline asked with a shiver. She didn't need to wait for Will's answer to know that it would be, "Yes."

The repeated, yipping calls of coyotes resounded in the otherwise quiet night as they headed back to the Circle-L. Will nudged his horse into a trot. "Faster," he told Emmeline.

"This horse is too tired," she argued.

"I said, faster." He flicked the loose ends of his own reins against her horse's rump, and the animal picked up the pace.

"What are you doing?" She frowned at him.

"Well, I'm not abusing these animals, if that's what you're thinking. Don't you hear the calls?"

"You mean the coyotes? Sure. Why?"

"Because, unless I miss my guess, those aren't real coyote howls."

She gasped. "Indians?"

"Most likely. And they're closing in. Listen."

To Will's chagrin, the noises repeated, this time even nearer. "They must be on horseback or they wouldn't be catching up to us so fast."

"What should we do?"

"Ride," he shouted, glimpsing a slight movement in the long grasses to his immediate left. "Now!"

He kicked his sorrel hard and saw Emmeline do the same to her mount. If he'd had any doubt of her prowess as a rider it was quickly dispelled. She rode like the most adept cowhand, leaning into the wind and perfectly in tune with her horse.

If he hadn't been so worried about eluding the Indians, he'd have complimented her then and there. As things stood, however, their first task was escaping. Lord willing, there would be plenty of time later to exchange pleasantries.

Will's horse started to pull slightly ahead and he had to slow to keep from leaving Emmeline behind. Since they didn't know which Kansa clans were involved in the chase, there was no way for him to predict what might happen if those Indians did manage to overtake them.

He dropped back just far enough to take another swing at her horse's rump with his loose reins and deliver the necessary impetus. When they got home he'd give both horses an extra ration of grain and a rubdown to make up for pushing them so hard.

As if on cue, Emmeline began to kick her mount harder. She loosened the reins to give it its head and let it race freely, choosing its own path across the high plains.

Will was secretly pleased. She not only understood the danger, she was trusting the horse to find the best way home. He could not have asked for more.

"How much farther?" she shouted.

"About a mile. They won't follow us all the way. We're almost in the clear."

He saw her glance over her shoulder. "Oh? I think somebody forgot to tell *them*."

When Will turned, he was astounded to see that there were at least six riders closing in. He couldn't let them catch Emmeline. Even if he had to stop and hold them off single-handedly, they must not overtake her.

He drew his pistol, aimed into the air over his opposite shoulder and fired.

"What are you doing?" she screeched. "Do you want to make them *really* mad?"

"I'm not trying to shoot anybody. I just want to scare them off."

"Is it working?" she asked, her voice made shaky by the galloping of the horse.

Will chanced another look. His heart soared. He

waited a few moments before he answered, "Yes. They're falling back."

"How long do we have to keep riding like this?"

"Till we can see the ranch house and my men are within shooting distance," Will answered. "You okay?"

"Yes. But the next time we come out here I'm going to be armed, too," she replied decisively.

He knew better than to argue with her. Later, when she'd calmed down and was thinking more rationally, he'd probably be able to reason with her and talk her out of running around on the plains unescorted, let alone with a firearm. That was a man's job—*his* job—to keep her safe, to take care of her.

The instant that thought popped into Will's mind he knew he'd better not voice it to Emmeline Carter. Not if he wanted that apple pie she'd promised, not to mention keeping her on as his cook. He could envision the fire in her eyes and the expression of disgust on her pretty face if he so much as suggested that she was not capable of taking care of herself, and her family as well. He'd never met anyone, man or woman, so determined to be independent, and to answer to no one.

His gut twisted uncomfortably at that obvious conclusion. Thanks to her father's overbearing influence, Emmeline would have a hard time believing in any man's ability to make her happy and keep her protected. She'd turn down marriage in a heartbeat if it meant sacrificing her independence.

Not that it mattered to him. He wasn't personally interested in the likes of her, of course. As he'd often told Zeb, he was either going to remain a bachelor forever or eventually look for a nice widow woman whose children were already raised.

He knew better than to chance becoming anyone's father. His own father, and his father before him, had been notoriously cruel.

Will was not about to put himself in the kind of situation that might bring out those same faults in himself. As his mother had often said, "The apple doesn't fall very far from the tree."

Will finally slowed his lathered horse, but insisted they continue to ride side by side the rest of the way home. To his relief, his companion didn't argue. After the scare she'd just had, he wasn't surprised, although it would have been totally in character for Emmeline to have balked at any suggestion she thought might be an order, no matter how sensible.

"There's a light in the window. Looks like your family waited up for you," he said.

"I hope so. I want to show them all the ribbon."

"Do you think that's wise?"

"Why not?"

"I was just thinking of Bess. You said she was a bit better and I thought perhaps it would be best to save the ribbon for later instead of shocking her unnecessarily. It won't change anything."

"Of course it will. It will tell us which direction Missy went."

"Only if it stayed in her hair during the tornado and she left it behind later, as a clue. You have to admit, it's a lot more likely the ribbon got blown loose in the storm. It might not even be the one she was wearing—it could have just been an extra ribbon that got scattered with all the rest of your belongings."

He dismounted in the yard and held the bridle of Emmeline's winded horse so she could get down safely. When he noticed that she seemed a bit unsteady, he shouted for Clint to come and take the horses so he wouldn't have to leave her.

"Walk them out, give them a good rubdown and feed them as soon as they've cooled down," he told the lanky cowboy.

"What happened, boss?"

"Indians. Post a guard tonight, just in case. Use Hank for the early-morning shift. He's used to being up before daylight, anyway, so he shouldn't have any trouble staying awake."

"Right."

As Clint led the horses toward the barn, Will continued his conversation with Emmeline. "Do you really think Missy might have left the ribbon there on purpose?"

"I don't know. Maybe. I can only remember scattered details about being caught in the storm, so I doubt an eight-year-old would be calm enough to plan ahead. Not at a time like that."

"True," Will said. He saw her arch her eyebrows and roll her eyes as he opened the door for her.

"*Now* you agree with me? Why?"

"Because this time you're probably right."

"Probably?"

The look of exasperation on her face was so amusing he had to fight the urge to smile. There was nothing humorous about the situation, yet everything Emmeline said or did seemed to please him unduly. To say that that was a strange reaction, especially for him, was to understate the subject greatly. In the space of mere days, this young woman had breached the stone wall he maintained around his emotions and had become a part of his life. He looked forward to seeing her, conversing with her, even arguing with her. She gave as good as she got and was an intelligent adversary in many areas, not the least of which was logic.

Except for her obsession about those missing children, he added to himself. He certainly couldn't fault her for that. He was worried, too. He had lived in High Plains long enough to know that the chances of anyone finding hide nor hair of the twins, dead or alive, was lessening by the minute.

Chapter Ten

Emmeline felt compelled to pause on the porch to scrape the mud off her shoes while Will did the same to his boots. Although the floor of the ranch house was made of bare planks, she still wanted to keep it as clean as possible, especially since she and her mother had worked so hard to sweep it clean after they'd arrived.

Joanna, recovering her health at an amazingly rapid rate, was alone in the tiny parlor, occupying the only rocking chair. She arose and greeted Emmeline with a brief hug, then stepped back to study the younger woman's expression.

"You found them, didn't you?" she asked in a near whisper.

"No." Emmeline reached into the pocket of the oversize coat, withdrew the short length of pink ribbon and held it up. "But I did find this. Do you think it was Missy's?"

Joanna Carter swayed slightly, then dropped back into the chair. "I don't know for sure. I suppose it could be hers. If I still had my sewing basket I could tell you. I had a spool of ribbon like it."

"Well, I think it's hers," Emmeline said flatly. "I'm going to proceed on that premise. Mr. Logan… I mean, Mr. Will…and I will go back in the daylight and see if we can find any more clues."

"That was all you found, all you saw, tonight?"

Emmeline could tell that Will was waiting for her to disclose her encounter with the Kansa brave and he was obviously taken aback when she refrained from doing so.

Their gazes met and she knew Will read her meaning. She did not want him to say anything else, and hopefully he would hold his peace.

He nodded, letting her know he understood, and she rewarded him with the hint of a smile.

"If you think you can get away from the kitchen after the midday meal tomorrow, we'll ride out then," he said. "If not, we'll try to get an earlier start after supper."

"Maybe we can do both," Emmeline said. She looked to her mother. "Where's Bess?"

When Joanna turned to face the doorway leading to the bedroom, everyone followed her gaze. Bess was standing there, staring at Emmeline. Her eyes widened at the sight of the ribbon in her hand. She wavered, leaning a shoulder against the doorjamb to steady herself.

"I told you to be careful," Will said quietly. "Get rid of that thing."

Emmeline wadded up the slim, pink ribbon and stuffed it back into her coat pocket. "It's all right, Bess," she said. "I was just going to ask you if you could help me with the meals again tomorrow. Mr. Will and I have to leave for a while and the bread may not be done by then. Can you mind it for me and take it out of the oven?"

The fifteen-year-old nodded, but her eyes were glassy, as if she were not really seeing, and she stumbled as she turned and walked back into the bedroom. Joanna bustled after her, obviously concerned.

"I think you got away with it," Will whispered from behind Emmeline.

He took a stagger step back when she turned, put out her hand and opened her fist to show him what she was holding.

"That's not all I got away with," she said. "Look what I just found in my pocket. It must have fallen in during the—the *accident*. What shall I do?"

The sight of the tarnished button clearly unnerved him. "You didn't pick it up?"

"No. Of course not." She lowered her voice even more. "Maybe he won't miss it."

"I wouldn't count on that," Will replied, scowling. "He probably had a reason for every one of those trinkets. That looks like U.S. Cavalry issue. It may have come from one of their uniforms."

"I shudder to think how he might have gotten it. I thought you said these local Indians were peaceful."

"Yes, and no," Will answered, eyeing the bedroom doorway. "That blanket you ladies hung across the opening won't keep sound from penetrating. I think we should step outside if we're going to continue this conversation. I want to tell you a few more things about the history of this area."

Emmeline shivered but let him escort her the rest of the way onto the porch and close the door behind them before she asked, "Is it bad?"

"Depends which side you're on. Around this same time last year, they hung the son of Fool Chief and another Indian, over in Council Grove."

"Why? What did he do?"

"Not all that much. The Kansa were just being themselves. They'd stolen a couple of horses from a Mexican freighting company that was bringing goods to a Council Grove merchant. When the Indians heard how upset everyone was, they rode into town to give the horses back. After that, one thing led to another."

"Oh, dear."

"That's an understatement. Returning the stolen horses seemed like a successful gesture of goodwill on the Indians' part until somebody started a fight.

Shots were fired and two townspeople were wounded. It could have been much worse. There were over a hundred Kansa in the visiting party. They could have easily slaughtered the settlers."

Her hand flew to her throat. "Was anyone actually killed?"

"Not then. The Indians withdrew. That would have been the end of it if the law hadn't insisted that they send the guilty parties back to face trial for shooting in the first place, even though it was in self-defense."

"Is that when the chief's son was executed?"

"Yes. And Fool Chief swore vengeance. Nothing has come of his threats yet, but I'm sure we haven't heard the last of him. If he'd been nearby when you screamed, I doubt he would have turned tail and run."

"Maybe it was him who chased us."

"That's what I was thinking. That's why I need to be certain you're taking my warnings to heart."

"Such as?"

"I know you want to continue your searches, but you need to remember the dangers. If you act too boldly, too carelessly, there's no way I can hope to protect you. Do you understand what I'm trying to say?"

Emmeline looked up at his handsome face, haloed by the lamp inside. "Yes. The Indian might have wanted an eye for an eye, the way the Good Book says."

"That's right," Will replied. "He might have killed you on the spot and seen it as the only fair thing to do. If he finds you out there again, there's no telling what he'll do, especially if—" he pointed to the button in her hand "—he thinks you stole his trophy."

All she could do was gape at him in reply. Truth to tell, he might have said those things merely to make her listen to his admonitions, but she doubted it. Will Logan was not the kind of man to purposely frighten anyone. If he was that worried about the Indian threat, then she should be, too.

Suddenly shaky, she swayed closer to him.

Will put out a hand to steady her.

She leaned toward him, expecting him to at least slip his arm around her shoulders the way he had when he'd rescued her on the prairie so recently.

Instead, he put her firmly away from him. "You should go inside and check on your mother."

If Emmeline had not heard a slight tremor in his voice, had not sensed his emotional response to their closeness, she might have thought he was rejecting her. Clearly, that was not the case. Will Logan was as moved by their sense of companionship as she was!

While in her deepest heart she hoped she was not imagining things, she was also concerned for his feelings. Had she unknowingly led him on? Made him believe she was eager to be courted when she was not? She had certainly not intended to do so.

The problem seemed to be rooted in the strange feelings that surfaced whenever she was around him. Emmeline found herself looking forward to being near Will, even briefly. She'd lost count of the times she had stepped out onto the porch to scan the yard or had peered into the distance, hoping to catch the merest glimpse of the handsome rancher.

Admitting as much, even to herself, was terribly unsettling. She knew nothing must take precedence in her life but the cares of her family. She'd felt that way from the time she was old enough to begin helping Mama. And Papa's temper and spiteful ways had further convinced her. She had vowed she would never be foolish enough to fall in love or consider marriage and she wasn't about to rethink that decision while embroiled in the midst of the current crisis.

When it was over and life got back to normal, would she change her mind? she wondered. If she'd been able to banish the image of Will's face from her thoughts, her resolve to stay single might have been a lot stronger.

The following day seemed to creep by for Emmeline. She had churned butter right after break-fast, then put the copper boiler on and scrubbed more clothes, hanging them on a heavy wire line to dry while she started the bread rising.

Bess was acting as if the shock of seeing the

ribbon had not caused her to relapse so there was that to be thankful for, in a manner of speaking. At least the dirty, wrinkled ribbon had apparently not aggravated her condition the way Will had warned it might.

And speaking of Will, Emmeline hadn't seen him since he'd come in after his morning chores and eaten a big meal with the rest of his men.

She'd been surprised to note that the other cowhands had already started treating Johnny as one of them, teasing him and clapping him on the back the way they often did each other. Since the young man had appeared to enjoy the friendly taunts, she had not interceded to try to mother him.

She had the bread in the oven and was getting ready to suggest that it was time to once again explore the site of the wagon wreck, when movement outside caught her eye. She peered through the window. A rider was approaching. Maybe someone had found the twins! Drying her hands on her apron, she hurried outside.

Will had apparently seen the man coming, too, because he left the barn at the same time and joined her in the yard.

"This is Richard Preston, our pastor," Will told Emmeline.

She offered her hand as the gaunt, sober-visaged man dismounted and greeted her. "Mrs. Carter?"

"That's my mother. I'm Emmeline. Have you found the lost children?"

"Sorry. No." He removed his black hat and nodded politely. "I came to offer my condolences and my services, miss. We have your father's grave dug and we're ready to proceed. I assumed your family would want to be present when he was laid to rest."

"Of course." She blinked and shaded her eyes from the bright sunshine to hide a rush of unexpected emotion. "I realize we should hurry, especially in this warming weather. I'll go tell Mama."

As she turned to go, Will called after her, "We can take the spring wagon again. I'll get Johnny. We'll leave as soon as you women are ready."

All Emmeline could manage was a wave in response. She had not dreamed that her father's interment would touch her emotions so deeply, but the mere thought of it had her near tears.

She supposed she shouldn't have been surprised to feel the loss. After all, Amos was her father, and Mama had loved him in spite of everything he'd said and done to her over the years. Glory would probably be upset, too. So would Johnny. And maybe, just maybe, the funeral would jar Bess into speaking, if only to sob along with the others. *Anything* would be better than her continued silence and that usually blank stare that was so unnerving to everyone.

"Mama," Emmeline called as she entered the ranch house. "Mama? Where are you?"

"In the kitchen, helping Bess with the bread,"

Joanna answered. "It's beautiful. Couldn't have done better, myself, not even on my best days."

"Thank you." Approaching cautiously, Emmeline waited until both Bess and their mother were away from the stove and had turned the loaves out of the pans and onto racks to cool.

"The preacher from town is here," she began, judging from her mother's expression that she immediately understood the reason for his visit. "They're ready. He just came to tell us so we could go into town for Papa's funeral."

"I don't have anything black to wear," Joanna mumbled. "I should have thought—should have planned..."

"No one will think ill of you for that, especially under such trying circumstances," Emmeline said. "Just grab your bonnet and a shawl. I'll get Glory ready."

Both women looked to Bess. She was acting no different than she might have if someone had just told her the sun was shining.

"Shall we leave her home?" Joanna asked Emmeline.

"I don't think that's wise. Not unless Johnny stays with her and I know he'll want to go."

"All right. We'll hurry and fetch our shawls, like you said, just in case we're late getting back."

As Emmeline watched her mother shepherding Bess from the room, she felt the full weight of her responsibilities. It was as if she was the parent and all the other members of her family were her wards. She was in charge. She had been ever since Papa had been killed. Mama was starting to recover, but there was still no respite in sight. Not unless the people in her life changed a great deal.

"Please, God," she prayed softly, "help me to help them, to do the right things and keep them safe and well."

Hardly were those words out of her mouth before she thought of Missy and Mikey again. Two other innocents had been in her charge and she had failed to protect them.

It didn't matter to Emmeline that the force of the twister had overcome everyone and everything. There must have been something she could have done, should have done. But what? How could she have kept them all safe when she, herself, was blown right out of the wagon bed?

It had been beyond her strength to fight the winds. But it had not been too hard for God to have intervened. And He had not done so.

As she led her littlest sister into the kitchen and washed her hands and face for her, Emmeline considered her Christian faith. In her deepest heart she still believed, still clung to God. But there was also a part of her mind that kept asking, "Why?" Why had God not turned or quieted the wind? Why had He left them so vulnerable? So alone.

Part of the disaster was because of Papa, his poor choices and stubborn nature, she concluded as she banked the fire, covered the fresh bread with a clean, dry cloth to keep the flies off and made certain the whole kitchen was secure.

Leading Glory to the door, Emmeline hung her apron on a peg, picked up her shawl, bonnet and reticule, then resolutely left the house.

"Where are we going?" the child asked.

"Into town."

"Is Mama going too? And Johnny and Bess?"

"Yes. Mr. Will is driving us, just like the last time."

"Oh, goody! I like him."

Emmeline sighed but made no further comment. It felt as if she were stepping into the future and leaving some intrinsic part of herself behind, which she was. When she and her family returned from High Plains in a few hours, their patriarch would be no more than a memory, buried in a cemetery in a town she had never heard of until a few days earlier. A piece of them all would lie under the Kansas sod and tie them to that area forever, whether or not they chose to stay.

Emmeline picked up the five-year-old so the friendly dogs wouldn't lick her face or get her muddy, balanced her on one hip and headed for the wagon where Will waited. The rest of her family was already ensconced in the back, so she handed Glory to her mother, then let one of the cowhands help her climb into the same seat she'd occupied before.

Will took the reins of the two-horse team.

"Where's the preacher?" Emmeline asked.

"He headed back to town so he can be ready when we all get there. A few of my friends are going to attend, too. I thought that might help."

"The only ones I really know are Cassandra and her brother," Emmeline said. "But thank you for being so considerate."

"They'll be there. And I've asked Clint to bring some extra horses into town so we can return this rig to Pete. I'm pretty sure he needs it."

"Thank him for us, please. And all of the others. I tried to be gracious when we were staying at the church, but I fear I was too concerned for my sister and the twins to have done a proper job of it."

"They don't expect special thanks. They were just being neighborly. Besides, you'll have a chance to repay their kindnesses soon, I'm sure."

"If we stay here instead of continuing with the wagon train," Emmeline said.

"Might you leave before we find the lost children?"

Her head snapped around and she scowled at him. "Of course not."

Seeming satisfied, Will flicked the lines over the backs of the team and they picked up their pace enough that Emmeline had to hang on to the bent-wire loop at the edge of her seat to restore her balance.

This ordeal will be over soon, she told herself. *And then what?*

What, indeed? Papa's funeral was necessary, of course, but it was only one small step in the restoration of her family to a normal life. They were on a journey with no signposts and no evident destination.

Her attention was drawn to the stalwart man seated beside her. Will Logan had been there when she'd needed him and had provided home and hearth. And she was grateful. It was thoughts of the future, of the unknown, that gave her pause and made her insides quake.

She realized that there was much she could never know for sure, such as why they were stranded or what awaited them as a family. Part of her kept imagining that they were at Will's mercy, while another part of her argued that only God could rescue them. If He would. It seemed wrong to question the faith she had leaned on for so long, yet when she had so many unanswered questions, when so much tragedy had befallen them, doubts kept niggling at the edges of her mind.

She would have liked to believe that landing in High Plains and getting a job at the Circle-L was part of her Heavenly Father's plan for her and her family, but that didn't explain Papa's death or their near-destitute condition until she'd met Will Logan.

Will, again. Her thoughts kept returning to him and his kindness, his gallantry. Could he be the reason they had ended up in High Plains? Was he truly a part of God's infinitely wise plan?

That notion took her aback. It was possible, she supposed. Anything was. She was simply having trouble accepting that God might have actually dropped them in the middle of nowhere and cost them so much simply to introduce her to the handsome rancher.

How ridiculous. She dismissed the idea with a stubborn lift of her chin as her thoughts continued to whirl. So Will was handy. And he had helped and protected her. Fine. That did not make him extraordinary. It simply meant that he was behaving in a gentlemanly manner. The whole town had come to their assistance, as was being further evidenced by the preacher going out of his way to arrange a funeral for a stranger.

For Amos Carter. Emmeline swallowed hard as reality pressed in on her. *For poor, poor Papa.*

Thoughts were whirling through her head, none more or less sensible than any other. Emmeline was so confused she wanted to leap from the wagon and flee into the peace of the open prairie where she wouldn't have to face one more question, real or imagined. She had no answers, no conclusions that would help her bear whatever was to come. It was as if she were being torn asunder by the riot of emotions she had kept under control for the sake of everyone else. She had not wept, nor ranted, nor shed hardly a tear through it all.

Now, on her way to her father's funeral, she

began to realize how close she was to the edge of her ability to dampen down her feelings. To keep hiding her pain.

A solitary tear slid down her cheek and she averted her face so Will would not see. If God did not love her, if He was not in charge of the universe as well as the lives of his children as she had always been taught, then she had no hope. None at all.

Silently calling out to her heavenly Father, Emmeline let her heart and soul do the kind of praying that her mind could not fathom. And, in the space of that prayer, she found the peace she had feared was lost.

Chapter Eleven

Will drove the wagon down the center of Main Street, nodding to acquaintances and taking care to avoid what little refuse remained along the wide roadway. Most of it had been cleaned up since the storm. There were still parts of roofs missing and visible damage to several buildings, including Pete's blacksmith shop, but the streets were pretty clear and most of the broken limbs from the cottonwoods had been hauled away, presumably to use for firewood. All in all, High Plains was showing more signs of early recovery than he'd expected.

Nearing the cemetery, he was amazed at all the people who had turned out for the services. A string of buggies and horses stood facing the cemetery, which was already crowded. Judging by the number of open graves, all the casualties resulting from the tornado were going to be buried at the same time. That made sense. There was no reason to drag it out.

Zeb and Cassandra Garrison were present. So was the dressmaker, Mrs. Morrow, and her daughter, Winnie. The Johnson family was there in full force, too. He noted that Rebecca Gundersen looked upset and assumed that Matilda Johnson must have said something unkind to her. That was unfortunately all too common for the shopkeeper.

Matilda's daughter, Abigail, was there as well, a sneering expression overshadowing the prettiness of her face. She had picked up many of her mother's nasty habits and was therefore, in Will's opinion, the second least likable person in town, her mother being the first.

He brought the wagon to a stop at the outskirts of the small cemetery. It had had few burials since its founding, but one was too many as far as he was concerned. When he had invited his friends and acquaintances to settle in High Plains he'd had only their best interests at heart. The untimely deaths of Pete Benjamin's wife and newborn baby had cut Will to the quick. Things like that were not supposed to happen to young people, and certainly not to innocent babes. Every death then had been hard to bear, but this was the first time there had been so many new graves at once. His heart ached for the family members burying loved ones, and most especially for the woman by his side.

He climbed down, tied the team to a hitching post and went back to help Mrs. Carter disembark while Zeb assisted Emmeline.

Cassandra immediately embraced her and he could tell that both women were dabbing at tears as they walked away together. He was touched by his old friend's compassion, knowing that the loss of her own parents gave her a special understanding of Emmeline's feelings. Cassandra was like a sister to him. Since the death of his parents, he'd considered her and Zeb his only real family.

Leaving his place at the rear of the wagon, Clint Fuller brought the extra horses forward and tied them at the same rail while addressing Will. "I'll take the rig back to Pete's for you, boss. Anything else you need while I'm in town?"

"No. Just bring the team back and then wait for us. I don't think this will take long."

He noticed that Clint was eyeing the assembling mourners and that his attention seemed to be focusing on Cassandra, as usual. Unfortunately, Will had heard that the young woman had set her cap for Percival Walker, the lawyer. Oh well, it wouldn't hurt Clint to dream. There weren't that many marriageable women in High Plains and therefore the competition for their favor was intense.

Clint didn't have a chance with Cassandra, of course, but Will couldn't help wishing the cowhand could give old Percy a run for his money. The attorney was a necessary part of High Plains workings, especially since there had been so much confusion over treaty lands and government control of them, but that didn't mean the man was likable.

On the contrary, Percival was the kind of fellow who used his handkerchief to dust off a chair before sitting in it and was so prissy he almost always wore white gloves and a fancy, citified suit and brocade vest, even on hot summer days. Percy always acted as if he was a cut above the rest of the townspeople and was lording it over them. Not that many of them, particularly the younger men, took him seriously.

Will sobered as he followed the small crowd of mourners to the first graveside where Reverend Preston waited. Joanna Carter was weeping audibly and several other women, including Emmeline and Cassandra, were comforting her while those same Tully brothers who had been such hooligans before, poked each other in the ribs and pointed to the grave, evidently enjoying a private joke at the expense of the deceased.

Standing back and removing his hat, Will overheard Matilda Johnson shrilly lamenting the fact that the Carter women were not suitably dressed for mourning.

Leave it to her, Will thought. He sidled closer.

"I'm so happy to hear you volunteering the goods for black dresses, Mrs. Johnson," he said aside, making sure he was overheard by as many others as possible without letting his voice travel as far as Emmeline and her kin.

"What?" Matilda's eyebrows arched and she stared at him as if he had just proposed something indecent. "I never—"

"They will be in to select something suitable in a few days, I'm sure," Will added. "And I'll pass the word about your generosity. I'm sure it will generate plenty of goodwill among your regular customers."

The portly shopkeeper spun on her heel, grabbed her daughter's hand and stomped off, dragging the young woman with her. Judging by the way Abe Johnson was hanging back, he wasn't looking forward to listening to his wife's coming tirade. Well, too bad. If that overly critical woman was going to spout off, it was only fair that she be forced to help correct whatever wrongs she was lamenting. And there had been plenty of them in the past.

Will almost smiled. It wasn't often that he got the upper hand with the Johnsons, and he was glad it had happened in a way that would benefit Emmeline and her mother. Even if they refused the fabric, or chose to take it and pay for it, the suggestion that it be an outright gift would vex Matilda for days. And now the Carters wouldn't have to listen to her petty, malicious criticisms during the funeral service.

As he watched respectfully, Amos Carter's plain casket was lowered carefully into the grave and Reverend Preston began to pray over it.

Will folded his hands and closed his eyes. Because he couldn't hear the reverend's words above the loud weeping, he prayed his own prayer for the Carter family. It wasn't fancy. Nor was it eloquent the way Richard Preston's prayers always were. But Will meant every word, every thought of his simple plea for the healing of their broken hearts.

His faith was stronger now than it had ever been and he wished mightily that he'd shared that with Emmeline when she'd expressed doubts. Everyone had those from time to time. It was the folks who clung to Christ through thick and thin who came out best, no matter what.

If he could have given her any gift, any advice, it would have been to look to God for solace.

"And help those lost children," Will added in a whisper. "Please, Father, watch over them, wherever they may be."

He didn't speak the thoughts that followed, but they were there, just the same. In his heart he had to add, "No matter what."

Emmeline took a hankie from her reticule and blotted her tears, then placed her arm around her mother's shoulders and guided her away from the site so she wouldn't have to watch the men shoveling dirt onto the simple pine casket and finishing the interment.

The preacher had stepped over to the next open

grave and begun to pray again. She wasn't sure who else had perished, but she hurt terribly for all those who had experienced losses.

A quick glance back at the assembled crowd told her that one of the other plots must be for Alex Henning's older brother, Eli. Ten-year-old Alex had been traveling with the only relative he had left in the whole world and was now standing next to an open grave, weeping uncontrollably, thereby making it clear what had happened. *The poor thing.* If she had not had her own family to worry about, especially Bess who was just standing there, staring blankly, she would have gone to the child and held him tight.

To her relief, a middle-aged woman seemed to be looking after him. As soon as Emmeline reached Will, she asked for details.

"Who is that older lady with the brown hair and plain dress? See her? She's looking after that sad little boy."

Will nodded. "That's Millicent Jennings. She runs the boardinghouse."

"Do you think she'll take good care of Alex? He has no other family that I know of."

"I'm sure she will. She not only has a kind heart, Zeb has arranged to pay her for looking after any and all new orphans from your wagon train until other arrangements can be made."

"Oh, good. I don't know how I could manage to care for anyone else, especially not now." Her gaze darted to Bess and lingered while she spoke softly to Will. "Nothing seems to faze my poor sister. I was hoping, once she saw all this, she'd snap out of it."

"Time will heal her."

"I certainly hope so. I've prayed and prayed, but…"

"That's an excellent first step."

Her eyebrows arched and she rolled her tear-reddened eyes at him. "As I said before, I'll reserve judgment on that." She didn't mean to be argumentative, but his apparently crystal-clear assurance of divine guidance was beyond her. There *couldn't* be a good reason for all that had happened. Even if she had been privy to God's infinite plans she would not have been able to accept these horrific losses.

The horses that Clint had brought were saddled and waiting, as was the one that Will had had tied to the rear of the spring wagon during their trip to town. Now she saw that the two-horse team was also present, although not prepared for riders.

"How are we all going to get home?" Emmeline asked.

"I don't have enough spare saddles for all of us. Clint and I will ride bareback. You and your family can take the other horses and one of you can hold Glory."

She stared at him, willing him to understand her underlying meaning when she added, "Is it safe?"

"In broad daylight, yes," Will said, resting his palm on the butt of one of the holstered pistols strapped to his belt. "Don't worry. Clint and I will take good care of you."

"I should tell Cassandra goodbye and thank her for coming," Emmeline said. "Will you stay and watch Bess and the others for me for a minute?"

"Sure. I'll get everyone mounted. Hurry back."

"I will."

She knew she was taking a chance, especially since she didn't know Cassandra that well, but she had to pose a question to her while she had the opportunity to do so.

Locating the other woman in the rear of the crowd that was gathered around the graves, she drew her aside. "May I ask a favor of you?"

"Of course. Do you need another dress? I may have one that would fit your mother."

"No, thank you. It's not that. I was wondering, I mean, I need…"

Cassandra took Emmeline's hand and patted it. "Don't be afraid to ask. I'll gladly do whatever I can to help."

"I—I need a gun," Emmeline whispered.

"What for?"

"Protection." She saw the other woman's gaze jump to Will and their party, so she quickly added, "Not against him. It's for Indians or wild critters or some such thing. I used to be armed all the time at home." The exaggeration tugged at her conscience, but she didn't alter or qualify her statement.

"I think I may be able to find you a little muff gun to carry in your reticule. Is that what you meant?"

"Not exactly, but it's better than nothing."

"What were you planning to do, run around dressed like one of these rough-and-tumble cowboys?"

"If necessary," Emmeline said boldly.

"In that case, why don't you ask Will for a gun?"

Emmeline felt her cheeks warm at the mention of his name. Worse, her new friend was staring at her and starting to get a funny expression.

"Oh, I see," Cassandra said, smiling slightly. "Will won't give you one."

"I haven't exactly asked him, but judging by the stern look he gave me when I mentioned wanting to be armed, I doubt it," Emmeline declared.

"You're positive he'd refuse?"

"Probably."

"Okay. I'll see what I can do. I'd been planning a trip out to the Circle-L anyway. I thought maybe, if I read to Bess, it might help her recover. Besides, I'm sure your youngest sister would enjoy hearing some stories, too. I doubt you have much free time to spend with either of them."

"That's been the case so far. I have managed to go searching for the twins, but that's the only thing I've done besides work in the kitchen and around the house. It was in terrible shape when I first stepped foot in it."

"I can imagine." Cassandra was eyeing the group

preparing to return to the Logan ranch as she spoke, and Emmeline saw evident personal interest.

Could she be sweet on Will? Emmeline wondered. Perhaps, though from what she'd seen, Will seemed to treat Cassandra like a sister. Perhaps she had set her cap for the cowhand, although in Emmeline's opinion, Clint Fuller couldn't hold a candle to his boss.

"Will you bring me the gun when you come to visit?"

Cassandra nodded. "Yes. And some bullets, although they'll be a tad hard to come by. Most of the men still use muzzle-loading revolvers and rifles around here."

"What do the Indians use?" Emmeline asked soberly. The look on her companion's face became solemn, serious.

"Have they shot at you?"

Answering honestly was, fortunately, possible. "Of course not. I just wondered if they used bows and arrows or firearms, that's all."

"I have no idea, thank the good Lord. And I sincerely hope I never find out." She once again looked past Emmeline's shoulder. "Will is getting impatient. You'd better go."

Giving Cassandra a parting hug, Emmeline turned and started back to her party, carefully hiking up her skirts and zigzagging to keep her shoes out of mud puddles as best she could.

A little muff gun, with its small-caliber bullets, was not going to help her feel much more secure. If she'd had such a weapon when the Indian had grabbed her, it might have only served to anger him, not deter him, especially if she had not delivered a fatal shot due to the size of the projectile. That was not good. Better to be sure of the stopping power of a larger caliber than to make a halfhearted effort and be sorry.

Could she actually shoot anyone? she wondered. If her life, or that of a loved one, was in jeopardy, she supposed she could pull the trigger. But she would never be the aggressor. That kind of thing was what foolish men did, like the ones who had started the fight with the Kansa in Council Grove. Others were still paying for their folly and might continue to do so for many years to come. Still, if the Indians were angry over the death of the chief's son, they'd attack her whether she was the aggressor or not. How could she put herself at risk like that again? But then…how could she *not* as long as the twins were still out there, at risk of being found and harmed due to the Indians' rage?

As she neared Will and the others, her thoughts lingered on the missing twins.

She allowed him to assist her into the saddle, then said, "It's still early. Can Clint take Mama and the children home while you and I swing by the old trail once more?"

He paused next to the horse. "Did you bring the button with you?"

"It's in my reticule."

"Then yes. I think that's a good idea. As soon as we locate the place where you found it, you can drop it and we can make tracks for home."

"I wanted to look for the twins, too," Emmeline said.

"We can do both. The most important thing is seeing that every bit of that necklace is put back where that Indian can find it."

"Suppose we can't locate the exact spot in daylight?"

"Then we have an additional problem," Will said with evident concern. "A big one."

Illuminated by the afternoon sun, the prairie looked altogether different than it had by moonlight. Will was pretty sure he could find the general area where he'd found Emmeline the night before again, but beyond that, who knew?

Still, he was bound to try for Emmeline's sake. Whoever the Kansa brave was, he would surely know if one of his trinkets was missing. The thought that he might come after her to reclaim it was too serious a consequence to even contemplate.

"Is it much farther?" Emmeline asked.

"I don't think so. How are you holding up?"

She huffed. "Honestly? I'm hot and tired and

I've cried so much my head is throbbing. In other words, I'm just fine."

Will had the urge to chuckle in spite of all that had transpired. When he said, "You remind me of my mother," and saw the look of astonishment on Emmeline's face, he did laugh.

"What's so funny?"

"You are. I was giving you a compliment."

"Thanks, I think."

"You're quite welcome." He reined in his horse closer to hers to continue the conversation. "Mother was the kind of person who always made the best of everything, even her life with my father."

"My mama did that, too."

"Except that you told me she took to a sickbed to escape." As soon as Emmeline nodded, he went on. "That's where you're different. You stood your ground and took care of your siblings, even though you were afraid of him."

"I was never—"

He saw the truth in her eyes and interrupted. "It doesn't matter anymore. That part of your life is over. But I understand how you feel because I went through the same thing. Even after my father was gone, the very thought of him still made me nervous. Then I felt guilty for being glad he couldn't hurt anyone again."

"How did he die?" she asked quietly.

"There was a house fire, back in Boston.

Nobody knows how it started, but both my parents were killed."

"I'm so sorry."

"Me, too. I've often wondered if things would have been different if I'd been at home when it happened. I suppose I should have stayed, for my mother's sake, but she'd given me her blessing and told me to leave, so I did. She even gifted me with her favorite diamond brooch."

"Do you still have it?"

"Of course. I wouldn't part with it even if I was starving, which I'm not, as you well know."

"Not yet, anyway. I just hope my family doesn't eat you out of house and home."

"You let me worry about that."

Will was glad for the distraction she offered. His memories of his last parting from his dear mother were so touching, so dear, he wanted to subdue them before he revealed too much. Emmeline needed a stalwart shoulder to lean on, not someone who put his own problems on display.

"Papa told me I couldn't leave until Glory was raised because Mama needed me," Emmeline said. "He may as well have saved his breath. I'd never have abandoned them."

"That's the kind of attitude I meant when I said you reminded me of my mother. You're a strong, capable, brave woman, Miss Emmeline. I'm proud to have made your acquaintance." He briefly pinched the front of the brim of his hat in a gesture of respect.

Although she blushed and made no reply, Will could tell his words had touched a chord. This was a woman wise and mature beyond her years, someone he could not only respect but admire greatly.

Besides that, she was good company. In spite of all she'd been through, she carried on and coped with everything life threw at her while maintaining a steady temper and a sensible outlook. He saw that as a rare gift, especially for a woman. He wouldn't dream of telling her so, of course. He was wise enough about female feelings to know better than to be too outspoken.

That didn't mean he didn't respect Emmeline Carter more than any woman he'd ever met, including Cassandra. Zeb's sister's allegiances were still half in Boston, half in High Plains. Maybe she'd never adjust to the more primitive lifestyle in the little town.

But Emmeline was all pioneer, from the toes of her high-button shoes to her bonnet. She belonged here, the way the sage grouse and buffalo herds did. They were an integral part of the landscape. The plains wouldn't have been the same without them.

And High Plains won't be the same when and if Emmeline moves on, Will told himself, sobering.

He hardly knew her, yet he was already certain he was going to miss her something awful if she left.

When she left.

Chapter Twelve

There was smoke coming from the stovepipe of the main ranch house when Emmeline and Will crested the ridge and once again looked down on the Circle-L.

They had managed to replace the Indian's tarnished brass button in what Will had assured her was the proper place, but had, unfortunately, not seen any more sign of the missing children. The only other folks they had encountered out there were a small search party whose continuing, tireless efforts had made Emmeline feel much better in spite of everything.

"Oh, dear." Emmeline pointed to the chimney smoke. "Look. I didn't realize how late it was or how long we'd been gone. Do you suppose Hank is back in the kitchen?"

"I sincerely hope not. He won't be if any of the

other hands have a say in it, that's for sure. They've all complimented you on the meals you've fixed."

"I thought they were just being polite."

Will's ensuing chuckle made her smile. That smile grew to a grin when he said, "They never told Hank they liked his recipes, no matter what he cooked up."

"I have had some problems finding the proper ingredients in your kitchen. Maybe you and I can go to the mercantile together soon and I can buy better provisions. Would that be all right?"

"*Very* all right."

Will was smiling broadly as they started down the slope toward the ranch and Emmeline felt an unfamiliar jolt of pleasure that he was so supportive, so empathetic. Her conscience immediately reminded her that she was supposed to be in mourning. Was it a sin for her to find joy in living when she had just bid a final farewell to her father? If so, she must be a terrible sinner, because she couldn't help her growing sense of contentment. The sun was warm but not too hot for comfort, the air was clean and fresh, the prairie was awash in wildflowers and she was riding beside someone who actually seemed to understand her. How could she not feel better?

The difficulty was going to be in explaining her mood to others, especially the older members of her family. Mama would mourn for the customary time, of course, and Bess and Glory hardly understood what had happened. But she and Johnny did.

One of the men in town had given the boy a black armband to wear as a symbol of his grief. On the other hand, the women in her family were expected to don somber clothing. Emmeline knew it was the right thing to do, but she wondered if she and her sisters could be excused. One of her biggest challenges was going to be making her mother understand her heartfelt wish to continue wearing crisp, bright calico instead of black.

Clint met them as they rode up to the barn. He spoke to Will and took charge of the horses while Emmeline hurried toward the house to resume her kitchen duties.

She burst in the back door, fully expecting to see Hank wielding a wooden spoon like a sword, ready to fight her off. Instead, Mama and Bess were tending the stove. Judging by the looks of the kitchen and the marvelous aromas, they had been cooking up a storm ever since they'd gotten back from town.

Emmeline laid aside her shawl, bonnet and reticule, then embraced them both in turn. "Something smells wonderful. What are you making?"

"Prairie chicken and dumplings with wild onions," Joanna said. "I know this is supposed to be your job, but Bess and I wanted to help." She glanced at the mute girl. "Didn't we, dear?"

To Emmeline's surprise, Bess looked up and

almost smiled. She still didn't speak, but the simple acknowledgment of having been spoken to was a big improvement over her previously catatonic state. And Mama was staying up and out of her sickbed. Would wonders never cease?

"Where did you get the hen?" Emmeline asked. "Did the dogs catch it or did Johnny shoot it?"

"Neither. One of the cowhands snared it and brought it to me right after we got home. I figured, with you being gone and all, it would be best to get it into a pot. I imagine it would be pretty tough and stringy if it didn't stew for quite a while."

Since there had been only two cowboys left behind when they'd gone into town for the funeral, Emmeline assumed their benefactor had been the one called Bob. That's why her jaw dropped when her mother said, "You know, I'd thought that old man was upset about us being here, but he seemed just as pleased as punch when he handed me that chicken."

"Hank? Hank gave it to you?" She grabbed a pot holder, lifted the lid of the Dutch oven and peered inside. "Are you sure this is a real prairie fowl? He didn't slip you a skunk, did he?"

"Of course not. I plucked that bird myself." Joanna was scowling. "What makes you say something so unkind and distrustful?"

"Oh, no reason." Emmeline's gaze met Will's as he entered the kitchen, his boots clomping hollowly on the plank floor. "You're not going to believe this. Hank fetched Mama a prairie chicken to fix for supper."

"Really?"

"Really," Joanna insisted, her hands fisted on her hips, her brows knitting over blue eyes. "What is the matter with you two? Hank seems like a very nice gentleman to me."

Emmeline and Will stared at each other for long moments before both began to smile.

"I never thought I'd see the day when old Hank was described quite like that," Will said, chuckling.

"I guess it's all in your point of view," Emmeline added. She took her apron from the peg by the back door and donned it, then turned to her boss. "Supper will be ready at the usual time, thanks to Mama and Bess. We'll ring the bell when it's time for you all to come inside."

She watched as Will doffed his hat to them and left. Seeing him go reminded her of what it was like seeing the sun set. The usual warmth faded. The brightness of the day waned. Shadows blanketed nature's splendor.

"I'm being silly," Emmeline muttered to herself. Yet her unsettling conclusions remained. When Will wasn't present she felt as if something vitally important was missing. What was wrong with her? She'd know him for mere days and already cherished his company as if they were dear old friends. Why?

Because he has helped me so much. And because

he truly understands my situation, she answered, unwilling to consider that there might be more to her emotional attachment than that. Foolish girls might entertain the notion that there was such a thing as love at first sight but not her. She might greatly admire Will Logan but she was not foolish. Nor was she a girl. She was a self-assured and capable woman, prepared to cope with every situation that arose.

Except for what has occurred in the past few days, she added, chagrined. For that, she craved an understanding ally. Like it or not, she needed Will Logan's help to survive, let alone thrive in the present circumstances. Perhaps she would continue to for weeks and months to come. Though that notion should have upset her, she found it comforting. And terribly worrisome.

Although Will had plenty on his mind, he couldn't stop fretting about the widespread tornado damage in town. That place was near and dear to him. It had taken them two long years to accomplish all they had in High Plains and their best efforts had been torn asunder in mere minutes. They would rebuild, of course. That went without saying. But it was distressing to consider all the work they had already put into the town and how much more would be required before it was restored to its former state.

When he'd run into Zeb outside the church and had briefly discussed rebuilding, they had agreed that the townspeople's welfare came first. Residences took priority. As soon as they had seen to the most crucial of those repairs, however, they'd start reconstructing the town hall, too. If all went well and they weren't hit with another summer storm or other such disaster, they should have it finished in time for the fall jubilee.

Will knew that preserving a sense of community was critical if High Plains was to continue to prosper, and he could envision a mass exodus if they failed to properly bolster town spirit. Perhaps there would also be a few of the wagon-train survivors who would decide to stay once they realized High Plains was a secure place to settle.

Like the Carter family. He immediately glanced back at the ranch house. Knowing they were living there was surprisingly comforting to him. It was as if he had finally found the family he had always yearned for. Even Johnny, who had been anything but cooperative to begin with, seemed to be adjusting. The boy reminded Will of himself at that age; holding others at bay by putting on the airs of a ruffian, yet lonely and lost inside until Zeb's family had shown him what love was like. Truth to tell, he liked Johnny. So did the other hands, even Hank.

That thought made Will smile. He was still

grinning when the objects of his musings rounded the corner of the barn together.

"You haven't been giving that poor kid any more of your homemade cheroots, have you?" Will asked the old man.

Hank snorted and spat aside. "Naw. He's learned his lesson about smokin', I reckon. Me and him's gonna go find us a good horse and train it some."

Judging by the way Johnny was grinning, he had no idea what Hank was really up to, but Will did. "If you were fixin' to put him on Lightning—don't."

"Aw, boss, he keeps sayin' he can stick on any horse we've got and I just wanted to see if he was braggin' or tellin' the truth."

"That's not the way to find out," Will insisted. "What would his ma say if you busted up her only son?" To his amusement the old ranch hand actually flushed under his ruddy tan.

"Give him a decent horse and take him with you to check on the new calves," Will ordered. "That's plenty of test of his ability, and it's necessary, to boot. No sense wasting his time or yours."

"Yessir."

Will addressed the boy. "And you do as Hank says while you're out there, you hear? Stay with him. He's boss when I'm not around. You got that?"

"Uh-huh."

His instructions had been as much for Hank's sake as for the boy's, and Will was relieved to see the older man take them to heart with evident pride as he shepherded Johnny toward the barn. That was precisely what Will had intended. As long as Hank felt in charge, he was less likely to try to educate Johnny inappropriately.

Will smiled to himself. The older man and the boy were likable characters. Different, but likable. Most of the folks who'd had the courage to test the plains were considered pretty peculiar by those who had stayed behind in the safety and peace of cities to the east. He, however, had never questioned his decision. Nor did he plan to return to Boston. Now that his mother had gone to Glory, Will had even less desire than before to see Massachusetts again.

Sighing, Will followed them to make sure Hank was taking his orders to heart. This was the only time in longer than Will could remember when thoughts of his late mother had not caused him lingering sorrow. He knew that no one would ever replace her in his heart, but he was also aware that he was looking forward to entering his home and being a part of the family housed there.

He'd employed the other cowhands for over a year and had enjoyed their company, such as it was. But had never realized or acknowledged how lonely he'd been until this very moment when the loneliness had passed, and he had someone inside the house whom he couldn't wait to see. Somehow, Emmeline

Carter had done what he'd thought was all but impossible—she'd turned his house into a home.

As soon as the chicken was done, the coffee brewed and the table set, Emmeline escorted Bess to the kitchen door where the dinner-bell triangle hung and handed her a metal rod.

"I'll show you how to do this and it can be your chore every day," Emmeline said, taking her hand to guide it. "Watch. You just put that metal stick inside this triangle and bang it around in a circle. See?"

The clanging made the girl jump, but she didn't flee.

"Now you try it."

Bess made a tentative effort, then backed away.

"That's fine for now. I see the men coming, so we know it was loud enough. Tomorrow, you can do it all by yourself." She smiled as Will, Bob and Clint approached. "Where's Hank? I thought he'd be Johnny-on-the-spot to taste Mama's stewed chicken."

Will nodded. "Me, too. Speaking of Johnny, I sent him and Hank to check on some newborn calves. They should be home soon."

"Are you sure?" As she wiped her hands on her apron she gathered a portion of it into a ball, trying to stifle her nervousness. "I don't like the idea of my little brother being out there like that."

"He'll be fine," Will assured her. "In all the time he's worked here, Hank has never missed a meal."

"That's hardly surprising since he was the cook." Emmeline made a face to emphasize her comment and was disgruntled when it made Will chuckle.

"Don't worry. As soon as they finish checking the herd they'll ride in and be starving. You'll see."

"All right. I suppose you know best," Emmeline said, but in her heart she wasn't nearly so sure. Johnny was impulsive and stubborn, and in spite of Hank's recent overtures of friendship, especially toward her mother, she still had doubts about his character. He'd been awfully angry when she'd usurped his kitchen duties and she couldn't imagine that he had mellowed in such a short time. Plus, he had been the one to offer Johnny a smoke and make him so sick. What could Will have been thinking when he'd sent the two of them out on the range alone? They hung around enough together in the course of daily chores.

She lifted Glory onto a chair and tied a napkin around her neck to serve as a bib before helping Joanna bring the meal to the table. No one seemed the least concerned that two members of their usual company were missing. Will and his men tucked into their bowls of stewed chicken and sopped up the extra gravy with chunks of fresh-baked bread as if they hadn't had a bite to eat for ages. Even Bess seemed to be enjoying the meal and Joanna was beaming under the profuse praise the men bestowed.

Only Emmeline remained on her feet. She paced

to the door and peered out, hoping, praying, to spot her brother and the old man. There was no sign of them. And the sun would soon set.

She paused beside Will and spoke to him in a whisper as she circled the table to pour refills of hot coffee. "I'm really getting worried."

"If they're not back by the time we finish supper, Clint and I'll ride out and have a look-see," he said.

Emmeline noted his casual smile at her mother as he spoke and how unconcerned he seemed. She also sensed an underlying tension. He might not be as apprehensive as she was, yet, but he was starting to be concerned.

She couldn't decide whether that was a good thing or if she should be even more anxious because of it. She didn't know Will Logan well, but she could tell enough to be certain that he was not nearly as untroubled as he was pretending to be. Was he keeping something from her? Or, was he still unsettled due to their earlier trouble with the Indians?

Thoughts of her encounter with the Kansa brave sent a shiver skittering up her spine. If he hadn't found the button and if he still believed she had stolen his talisman, perhaps he and his tribesmen had been watching the ranch, waiting for a chance to get even.

Her eyes widened. When she pictured Johnny as a prisoner of the Indians, perhaps tortured, or worse, her hand began to tremble so badly she had to put down the coffeepot to keep it from spilling.

She looked at Will, noting that he was studying her. His expression was solemn, as if he was reading her distressing thoughts.

He took one last swipe across his plate with his bread, popped the morsel into his mouth and pushed back his chair. "Bob, you stay here with the women-folk. Clint and I'll go see what that old codger is up to. He's gonna miss this delicious meal if he doesn't get a hustle on."

The lanky cowboy rose and followed Will out the door without comment. Emmeline's heart was in her throat. She faced the stove, closed her eyes and pled for deliverance for her brother and the others in silence. After all Mama and Bess had been through so recently, she doubted that either of them could stand losing another beloved family member.

Johnny is beloved, she affirmed, thinking of him fondly. He might be hard to get along with and too similar to Papa to be thoroughly likable in the last year or so, but he was still her only brother and she loved him. And had been doing so much better since they'd come to the Circle-L.

If he stayed on his current path, then once he was fully grown he'd be an enormous help to Mama, too, she added. He was finally learning to be respon-sible and trustworthy, now that he was away from Papa's influence. A man-child was always preferred over a girl, as Papa had often lamented. He'd toler-ated her, Bess and Glory while doting on his son and talking about Johnny as if he was the only one who counted. Of course, that kind of special treatment had gone to the boy's head. Such reactions were natural.

And now? Now, there was a chance that her brother wasn't ever coming home and all Emmeline could do was remember the times when, as a child, she had selfishly wished he had never been added to their family.

"Please, God," she whispered so no one else could hear, "forgive me. And bring Johnny back safe and sound."

Chapter Thirteen

Emmeline was still washing the supper dishes when she heard the ranch dogs barking to announce riders approaching. They were coming in at a gallop. Dismounting, Clint raced into the barn with the pack of dogs yapping at his heels.

She ran to meet Will and grabbed his arm. "What's wrong? Where's my brother? Is he all right?"

"He's fine." The rancher covered her hand with his before adding, "He and Hank met up with Cassandra. She was driving out to visit you this afternoon when her harness broke and left her stranded. Clint's going to go repair the rig for her and they'll all come in together. It shouldn't take long. She's not far off."

Emmeline was nearly overcome with relief. "Oh, praise God."

"I did," Will said, nodding solemnly. "If I hadn't

sent Hank and your brother out when I did, no telling how she'd have managed. I suppose Zeb might have come looking for her eventually, but he's been working at the mill from dawn to dusk ever since the twister hit. She left him a note, but it could have been pitch-black before he missed her and came looking."

Belatedly realizing that she was still gripping Will's arm and that he was patting her hand, Emmeline blushed and eased away. "She told me she'd come to visit, but I never dreamed it would be so soon."

"I was surprised, too," Will said, shaking his head. "I can't imagine what she was thinking. She's usually so levelheaded."

There was little doubt in Emmeline's mind why her new friend had acted rashly. Cassandra was obviously trying to deliver the derringer Emmeline had asked for and had risked being caught out of town late in the day in order to do so. That was not something she intended to confess to Will Logan, of course. It was bad enough that Cassandra might have prevaricated without complicating the situation by revealing more than was necessary.

"I'll tell Mama and the others," Emmeline said, sounding breathless. She attributed her unsteady condition to her fright regarding Johnny, rather than the fact that she had inadvertently touched Will's arm. The warmth of his hand atop hers still lingered and she could imagine feeling the muscles in his arm tensing, even through his shirtsleeve.

No wonder there were strong social prohibitions against such casual contact between a man and a woman, she mused. The effect of it was truly amazing. She was still trying to stop dwelling on the unsettling sensation of having felt his arm around her shoulders after the Indian encounter.

Grabbing a handful of skirt so she wouldn't trip, she hurried up the porch steps and into the kitchen where her mother and sister were helping clean up after the meal.

"They found Johnny and Hank," she announced. "They're fine. They'll be arriving soon. We need to set the table for three more."

"Three?" Joanna looked puzzled.

"Yes. Cassandra Garrison is coming for supper, too, and I imagine she'll have to stay the night since it's already so late. She can have my pallet."

"A fine lady like that? Nonsense. Glory and I will give her the bed and we'll sleep on the floor with you and Bess."

Emmeline didn't argue. She imagined that Cassandra would object to taking the only bed, but that was a moot point. What was most important was seeing that her new friend was safe and having a chance to converse with her in private about the pistol. Everything else was secondary.

* * *

When Will saw the party coming, Clint was driving Cassandra's calash-covered buggy. She was not only seated beside him, she appeared to be grasping his arm as if they were a courting couple out for a pleasant drive in the country.

Will met them and immediately confronted her the way he would have a misbehaving sibling. "What did you think you were doing? Have you lost your senses?"

"I was paying a neighborly call, that's all."

"Today?" He lowered his voice. "These folks just buried one of their own. Don't you think you should have waited a reasonable amount of time before intruding on them like this?"

"I'm not intruding," Cassandra said lightly and with a smile. "Emmeline invited me. Besides, I didn't come just to see her, I came to read to the other girls and entertain them while poor Emmeline slaves away all day in your hot kitchen."

"She works for me," Will countered. "It's not like I'm taking unfair advantage of her. I've given her whole family free room and board besides her wages."

Extending a gloved hand to him, Cassandra let Will assist her from the buggy, then faced him with aplomb. "I understand all that. Clint has assured me she's a wonderful cook, so you're benefiting, too. Right?"

"Yes. So?"

"So, make yourself useful and fetch those carpet-bags I tucked under the buggy seat, will you? That's a good fellow." Grinning, she turned on her heel and headed for the house. "I hope there's plenty of food left. I'm famished."

Will just stood there, staring after her and won-dering how he had managed to become a servant on his own spread. Leave it to Cassandra to make him feel as if he were about Johnny's age. If she did eventually settle on marrying Percival Walker, that slick, pompous lawyer was going to find out he'd met his match—and then some. It might be worth it just to watch Cassandra figure out ways to wrap that man around her little finger.

"Hand down those bags," he told Clint. "Then take her rig to the barn and stable her horse before you ride into town and tell Zeb she's staying here with us. I have a feeling we're going to be entertain-ing this houseguest for more than one night."

"Yessir. And a might pretty guest, if you ask me."

"Well, I didn't ask you," Will said flatly. "Cas-sandra's too friendly for her own good, so I can see why you'd think she's overly interested in you, but there's too much Boston left in her. Believe me, she'd never be happy on a ranch like this. Not for long, anyway, so don't get your hopes up."

The lanky cowhand was blushing as he passed the bulky carpetbags to his boss. "I still plan to ask her brother if I can court her. All he can say is no."

He swallowed hard, his Adam's apple bobbing with the effort. "You being his friend and all, what do you think my chances are of getting his blessing?"

Will shook his head and snorted. "Beats me. If Cassandra wants you to be one of her beaus she'll get her way, no matter what Zeb says. She won't mean to, of course, but all I can see ahead for you is disappointment."

"I'll take my chances," Clint said. "That lady is definitely worth it."

Lugging the bags to the house, Will was lost in thought. What made a sensible guy like Clint Fuller believe he had a snowball's chance in July of winning Cassandra's hand in marriage? And why her, of all people?

As far as Will was concerned, there was only one woman within a hundred miles worth bothering about. And she was so tied up in her own family responsibilities she might never decide to live a life of her own.

That's just as well, he assured himself. Emmeline Carter was young and vibrant, the kind of loving, nurturing woman who would surely want children of her own if she was to marry. And he was never going to become anyone's father. Never. The only kind of father he knew how to be was a bad one. Better to deny himself the comfort of a good wife than to choose one and then disappoint her because he made such an abysmal parent.

* * *

Emmeline and Cassandra greeted each other like long-lost siblings, being reunited after years apart instead of mere hours.

"How are you all doing?" Cassandra asked quietly.

"Much better than I had expected," Emmeline said, surreptitiously glancing at her mother and sisters. "Truth to tell, none of us have wept or carried on as much as I'd thought we would."

"That may catch up to you later. It took me months to finally come to terms with my parents' deaths and when I did, you should have seen the oceans of tears. But it didn't happen right away. I was beginning to think there was something wrong with my heart, if you know what I mean."

"I know exactly what you're saying. I've been kind of the same way. When Mama cried, I did too, but it was more for her than for Papa."

Cassandra removed her kid gloves and patted Emmeline's hand. "That sounds perfectly natural to me. It's your mother who needs the commiseration right now, not the one who has gone on to his eternal rest." Bustling past, she greeted Joanna and Bess, then bent to speak with Glory. "Hello, sunshine. How pretty you look this evening."

"What do you say?" Joanna prodded.

"I know?" The child giggled and hid behind her mother's skirts.

"No, you say, 'Thank you, Miss Garrison.'"

Glory parroted the phrase while remaining secreted in the full folds of Joanna's dress.

Cassandra's joyful laugh led the others to join in. "I can see this is going to be great fun," she said. "I had thought, since there's no school right now, you might allow me to tutor your little one, Mrs. Carter. I assume the others have received enough education, but I also thought that perhaps Bess would enjoy helping me teach her sister the alphabet and numbers. What do you say?"

For a moment, Emmeline was afraid her mother would refuse the kind offer. She needn't have worried.

Joanna beamed and nodded. "We'd be delighted. Wouldn't we, girls?"

Bess made little noticeable acknowledgement. Glory ducked deeper into her mother's skirt, while Emmeline spoke on their behalf. "It will be wonderful. Miss Garrison is a real teacher, just like Johnny and Bess and I had back home in Missouri, so she knows lots of interesting things. She's from Boston, too. All the way up in Massachusetts. Imagine that."

The little blond girl peeked out and gave the others a wan smile as if testing their reaction. When everyone laughed even more, Glory started to dance around the kitchen and spin in circles.

"I think she's warming to the idea," Emmeline said. "Please. Come and sit down. We have plenty of food left from supper. You must be hungry."

"Well, *I* sure am," Johnny said, barging through the door, plunking himself down at the opposite end of the long, plank table and grabbing his fork.

Cassandra carefully placed her gloves in her reticule and removed her jacket to lay it aside before sweeping gracefully into a chair. Instead of immediately reaching for the bread, however, she folded her hands, bowed her head and began to offer a prayer of grace.

Seeming oblivious, Johnny lunged for the ladle in the kettle that his mother had just placed in the center of the table.

Before Emmeline could reprimand him, Joanna stepped up behind the boy and cuffed the hair at the back of his head, startling him and making him freeze with his hand outstretched.

Her brother looked so shocked, so disbelieving, Emmeline nearly chuckled. Not only had Mama rarely disciplined any of the children, she had never been permitted to correct Johnny. Now, as she shook her index finger at him then silently pointed to Cassandra, he folded his hands to mimic the teacher and bowed his head.

There was little chance the rambunctious boy was actually praying, but as far as Emmeline was concerned, this show of respect for his elders was an excellent start.

That, coupled with the way Will and his ranch hands had been expecting Johnny to behave himself, was going to make a big difference in the boy's life. Maybe there was hope for him yet. She certainly prayed so.

And as for herself? Emmeline sighed. She had most of her family intact, a warm home and good meals provided. What more could she want?

That was an easy question. She desperately wanted to find Missy and Mikey alive and well. And she wanted Bess to recover fully. Perhaps, if the latter occurred, Bess would be able to give them some clues as to what had become of the twins. Without her input, it was beginning to look as though they were never going to locate those poor lost tykes.

Emmeline was actually beginning to hope that the Kansa or some other tribe had taken them in, regardless of their temporary treatment at the Indians' hands. If not, it seemed unlikely they could have survived this long without being found by any of the search parties. Better to have been fed and nurtured, even by so-called savages, than to have been left to die, alone, afraid and abandoned, on the unforgiving prairie.

Cassandra didn't stay only that one night. She lingered for nearly a week. When it came time for her to finally take her leave, Will could tell that Emmeline felt the loss strongly. She looked so crestfallen, in fact, that he invited the other young woman to tarry.

Cassandra laughed lightly. "I would love to stay longer, dear Will, but I have engagements in town. Percy has offered me a ride in his fancy surrey, all the way up to Manhattan, so I can visit the milliners there and buy a new hat, just like the ones in Paris. I'm surprised he hasn't already come looking for me."

"He's probably scared to make the trip alone," Will taunted. "Probably expects you to protect him from the Indians." He sobered. "You are carrying that gun I gave you, aren't you?"

"Well, not exactly. I've temporarily misplaced it," she said, darting a glance toward Emmeline as if asking forgiveness for not telling the truth.

"Then find it," Will ordered. "You know better than to be driving unescorted in the first place. Coming all the way out here unprotected is clear foolish."

"Perhaps you should have Clint escort me back to town," Cassandra drawled as she stepped off the porch toward her waiting buggy. "I'm sure he won't mind."

"I'm sure he won't." Will motioned to the cowhand who had been loitering in the background, making calf's eyes at Cassandra. "Saddle up. You're riding shotgun on this lady."

"Yessir!"

His unbridled enthusiasm made Cassandra giggle. So did Emmeline. "I have a feeling he doesn't mind," she informed her new friend. "I told you he liked you."

Will chimed in. "And I told Clint he didn't have

a chance with you, Cassandra, so don't toy with his affections. It's cruel."

"I'm not toying with him and I'm not pretending. I just haven't made up my mind about settling down yet," she countered, flouncing up to the buggy and letting Will help her in.

She seated herself and opened her parasol to ward off the sun in spite of the calash that already partially hooded it. "You said yourself it's not safe for me to drive around unescorted and unprotected. I think you should have Clint drive for me. He can tie his saddle horse on behind so he has a way home."

Emmeline was laughing, much to Will's consternation. "All right. He can see you home. But I'm warning you, Cassandra, if you do anything that costs me the best cowhand I've ever had, I'll take it out of your hide."

"I'd like to see you try," she retorted.

Although their exchange had been all in fun, Will could see that Emmeline was beginning to take his make-believe threat too seriously. That made sense. Her father had been the kind to really terrorize and then follow through. It was liable to be a long time before she could hear such innocent conversation and accept the fact that it was spoken in jest.

And, as he saw it, it was up to him to help her heart and soul find healing. He just wondered what he was going to do to protect his own.

Chapter Fourteen

As the days and weeks passed, Emmeline grew more and more restive, so much so that even strumming her dulcimer failed to calm her. The music was the same beautiful, plaintive strains as always. It was she who had changed. She wasn't sure what exactly was wrong with her, but she was beginning to suspect that her burgeoning affection for Will Logan was at the heart of her disquiet.

And it wasn't only she who had changed. Bess seemed to be coming back to life, although her progress was painfully slow. And Johnny had been spending more and more time with Will, and with Hank, so much so that the boy was actually beginning to sound like he meant it when he said, *Yes, ma'am* and *Yes, sir.* That improvement, alone, was amazing.

To Emmeline's further surprise, they had been practically stumbling over Hank in the kitchen whenever he had a free moment, and it looked as if he had eyes for her mother! Not that Mama would ever consider remarrying, of course. Many a time, she had insisted that once was enough.

The only member of their family who seemed unperturbed by all the changes was Glory, who was ever happy and carefree, especially when she was given a chance to play with the ranch dogs.

Wanting to speak privately with Joanna, Emmeline sent the little girl outside to do just that.

She found Joanna in the small parlor, once again seated in the wooden rocker. This time, she was darning socks for Johnny. Her Bible lay on the lamp table beside the chair.

Joanna looked up and smiled. "Hello, there."

"Hello. Do you have a moment? I'd like to ask you something."

"My, my, so serious." She laid the darning egg in her lap along with the floss. "Of course. I always have time for you."

Nervous and unsure as to where to begin, Emmeline blurted out her main question instead of leading with preliminaries. "How did you know you were in love with Papa?"

Joanna folded her hands in her lap as she gave her eldest daughter a pensive look. "At the time, I was told not to worry about such matters. That the woman wasn't the one to decide such things, and that I should accept whatever fate brought to me."

"Oh, surely not."

Taking a shaky breath and apparently phrasing her reply carefully, the older woman nodded. "Yes. That was what my parents raised me to believe. I married young, much younger than you are now, and my mother and father believed Amos would be a good husband. Amos was very much like my father."

When Emmeline opened her mouth to protest, her mother silenced her with a raised hand. "Hush. We will not speak ill of the dead. Your father provided well for us. He kept a roof over our heads and you children clothed and fed, even when I was so ill."

That was more than Emmeline could stand. She interrupted before her mother could go on. "He abused you terribly, if not always with his hands, then with his words. I hardly ever saw you smile until recently. Papa had a cruel streak a mile wide and you know it. He got worse as he got older, too, especially after Glory was born."

Joanna lowered her gaze. "Part of me believes that that was my fault. Men have needs. I was no longer able to satisfy my husband the way a wife should. Does that mean he had the right to be harsh or hurtful? I just don't know. Not anymore. There never was anyone to talk to me about love. I was told that a woman had duties, pure and simple, and if she failed to carry them out to her husband's full satisfaction, then she was a failure." A solitary tear rolled down Joanna's cheek and dropped into her lap.

"Oh, Mama, you're not a failure. You've been a wonderful mother," Emmeline insisted. To her relief, Joanna seemed to agree.

"I'm beginning to see that," she said with a slight smile, her cheeks flushed. "It has taken a tragedy to show me, but I am truly grateful."

"You mean because you're not so ill anymore?"

That question made the older woman giggle behind her hand. "Not exactly."

"Then what? What has happened?"

"Nothing, yet," Joanna said, grinning, and blinking away the remnants of the tears that no longer welled. "But perhaps you have noticed that I have a suitor."

"Who, Hank? I'd hardly call him *that*," Emmeline argued.

"Well, I would. And I can't say I mind awfully much. It's flattering to be courted, even if I decide that nothing must come of it."

"Because you worry he'll be just like Papa was?"

Joanna sobered. "I don't know. I may have been a married woman for many years but I really know very little about men. I don't suppose you could advise me?"

"Dear me, no! I was hoping you could do that for me."

"Afraid not, dear. I guess we'll both just have to muddle through." Her cheeks colored more. "I do think that Mr. Logan is growing fond of you, though."

Emmeline sighed. "That's what I'm afraid of."

Afraid was right, she concluded, giving her mother a kiss on the cheek and bidding her a tender goodbye.

How anyone could have tolerated Papa's abuse and still have wanted to cater to his every whim was beyond Emmeline's imagination. It made her even sadder to realize how her mother's upbringing had conditioned her to expect such ill treatment.

However, her mother was having a new experience now. Emmeline was glad that Mama finally had a chance to be treated well, and valued. She remembered how she and Will had smiled to hear Mama describe Hank as a nice gentleman, but when Emmeline saw the two of them together, she started to see what her mother had meant. Hank *was* a gentleman with her. And what's more, he treated her like a lady. But the budding courtship between them was too new to answer Emmeline's questions in regard to a person like Will. What kind of man was he, truly? How far could she trust him? She had seen him lose his temper a time or two. Did he have the potential to turn into a tyrant like Papa?

She wanted to make a rational choice and not rush into anything as Mama had with Papa, but how rational could she be when she was so eager to catch even a brief glimpse of him? When the sound of his deep voice sent shivers zinging up her spine and made the hair on the nape of her neck tickle?

He seemed to like her, too. He'd certainly treated

her with the utmost respect at all times, although in recent days he had grown a bit more distant.

"What I need is another opinion," Emmeline concluded. The next time she saw Cassandra, which would probably not be before church on Sunday, she was going to take her aside and ask. The Boston-born schoolteacher had never been a bride, of course, but she was far more worldly and educated than anyone else Emmeline knew, so her opinion would have to suffice. Besides, Cassandra had known Will for years.

In her heart of hearts, she hoped and prayed that Cassandra was not going to affirm the fears that kept Emmeline from reaching for happiness, because if she did, Emmeline feared her own spirit of hopefulness would shatter into a thousand useless pieces. And so would her tender heart.

Will had been escorting Emmeline, as often as possible, to continue to search for the twins. He had also been making regular forays into High Plains, like today, to assist in the rebuilding. Now that he had Hank back in the saddle and managing the other cowhands, his job had been simplified.

There would be times, such as during the fall roundup, when all riders would be needed, but this early in the summer there wasn't a lot to do except a little branding and ear-notching of the new calves. Hank could handle that without his oversight. And that meant that Will had time to ride out to the mill to talk to Zeb.

The Garrison Mill and cutting yard had been cleaned up nicely, although not entirely rebuilt. Zeb's first runs had gone to others in greater need and while work had slowed down for Will, the mill was still as busy as ever.

Reining in near the office, Will hitched his horse and went to find Zeb. He found his friend covered in dirt, flecks of bark and sawdust when he finally located him amid stacks of newly sawn lumber.

Will chuckled. "Whew! I see you're busy."

"When have I not been?" Zeb said, mopping his brow with a bandanna. "I've got my whole crew working a full day, except on Sundays, of course. We're finally starting to get a handle on everybody's rush orders."

"You know you can wait on anything for me," Will told him with a grin as they shook hands.

"Yeah. By the time I do get around to it, you'll probably be wanting to add onto your house, too."

"My house? What makes you say that?"

"Oh, just things my sister has mentioned."

Will frowned. "What's Cassandra been telling you?"

"Nothing, nothing." Zeb's grin spread till the corners of his eyes crinkled with glee.

"Okay, so maybe the Carter family is going to stick around, especially now that most of their wagon train headed west last week without them. If they do decide to stay in High Plains, I suppose I could consider building them their own house."

"Especially if you and Miss Emmeline tie the knot."

"Whoa. Who said anything about marriage? Certainly not me."

"Have it your way. But you're not getting any younger and she does like you."

"She does? Is that what your gossipy sister said?"

"Maybe. Maybe not. If you have doubts, why not ask Emmeline yourself?"

Will kicked the toe of his boot into a pile of sawdust to stall for time and carefully consider his reply. "Because she might say yes, and that would be the worst thing that could happen."

"How so?"

"I told you I was never going to marry unless I found a widow whose children were raised. I'm no father."

"Then marry Emmeline's mother," Zeb joked, laughing and giving Will a playful punch in the shoulder. "Problem solved."

"I don't happen to be in love with Mrs. Carter," Will said, dodging another punch.

"But you are in love with Emmeline?"

Will winced. "Yeah. Unfortunately, I'm pretty sure I am. I just have no idea what I'm going to do about it."

"Don't you think you're being a little too hard on yourself?" Zeb asked wisely. "Your father may have been a bully but I've never seen that side of you."

"Yet," Will said. "I just keep remembering Dad and Granddad. They were both hard to live with, especially in family situations. My poor mother suffered terribly."

"All the more reason why you know better than to let yourself emulate them," his old friend said. "Step back. Take your time. You'll see."

"Maybe. Maybe not."

"Just promise me you'll think about it."

Will huffed. "I've thought of little else since Miss Emmeline and her kin waltzed into my life and turned it upside down."

Emmeline had noticed that Will seemed to be going out of his way to avoid her of late. Could she be imagining things, be giving undue weight to normal actions simply because she was upset and confused? Perhaps. Or, perhaps he had sensed her disquiet in his regard and it had offended him. Would a kind, thoughtful gentleman behave in that manner?

There was no decisive incident she could recall that may have caused him to withdraw. Were all men so unpredictable? Her mother certainly seemed to think so.

Confusing thoughts continued to vex her to the point where she wanted to scream in frustration.

She'd tried to speak privately with Will, again and again, but he always had an excuse why he was not available to stop and chat.

Well, fine, Emmeline told herself. Since he wouldn't talk to her, she'd ride into town and visit Cassandra. If she took a packhorse she could also shop at the mercantile again and bring back whatever supplies the ranch kitchen needed, not to mention the spool of black thread Mama wanted so she could finish stitching the hem of her second mourning dress.

Removing her apron and smoothing the skirt of her pale blue calico, Emmeline gave thanks that her mother hadn't insisted they all wear somber clothes. With all the other stress already pressing in on her, Emmeline feared that being forced to wear such depressing colors would have fully unhinged her. Something was certainly wrong with her thinking, her mood. One minute she felt happy and the next she was either confused or fighting to keep from sulking or weeping.

The week's bread was baked and supper was simmering on the back of the stove. Will was in town, and Mama and Glory were napping. Therefore, Emmeline chose to simply write a short note and leave it on the kitchen table rather than stop to explain her reasons for leaving the house so abruptly. She supposed she couldn't have made her motives sound sensible if she'd tried.

She had no earthly idea why the urge to flee was

so strong or why she was acting on it, she simply knew she had to speak with Cassandra and there was no way she could wait until an upcoming Sunday.

"Besides," Emmeline added, hoping to reaffirm her decision as she grabbed her reticule and bonnet and headed for the barn to saddle a horse, "if I wait until I go to High Plains for church with my family and all the others, I'll never have an opportunity to catch Cassandra alone."

Privacy was crucial if she hoped to discuss intimate, womanly things as openly as she had with her mother. Just *thinking* about becoming a wife made Emmeline blush. It must be very difficult to choose to share your life with a man, yet most women did marry, so it couldn't be that bad. Certainly it wasn't as unpleasant for all as it had been for her mother.

"What if it is?" she asked herself as she slipped a bridle onto one of the more docile mares and buckled it behind the horse's ear. "Do I care enough for Will Logan to be willing to take that chance with the remainder of my life?"

Without hesitation, she answered, "Yes," and the surety of that one word made her tremble inside and left her heart pounding like the hooves of a stampeding herd of buffalo.

Emmeline stopped at Johnson's mercantile, left a list of supplies to be filled, then asked where she might locate Cassandra.

Abigail Johnson huffed and tossed her blond curls as if Emmeline had asked for directions to a saloon rather than a home. "Knowing Cassandra, she's probably holding court at her rich brother's."

"And that would be where?"

Pointing and shrugging, Abigail made a face. "West. Follow the mill road and you can't miss it. It's by far the biggest house out that way."

"Thank you."

Although the young woman's snobbish attitude was off-putting, Emmeline ignored it. All she wanted to do was see Cassandra and unburden her soul. She didn't care whether the directions to Zeb's home were given civilly or not, as long as they were accurate.

Taking Main Street west, she came upon an unmarked offshoot that seemed to lead toward the river, and assumed that had to be the road to the mill, particularly since several heavy wagons, loaded with stacks of trimmed lumber, were approaching from that direction.

In a few minutes, Emmeline caught sight of the three-story, whitewashed Garrison home. It was elegant, indeed. Even the yard looked more finished, more manicured, than any other place in High Plains. Although the wild roses along the front of the porch had obviously taken a beating from the severe weather and were still recovering, they were lovely. So were beds of other dainty flowers quite evidently transplanted from the plains.

She tied her horse and the pack animal to the hitching rail and stepped up onto the front porch. Little wonder this house was so well known, she mused. It was truly impressive.

Knocking, she was pleased when Cassandra quickly answered the door.

"Oh! Emmeline! What a wonderful surprise," Cassandra said, embracing her warmly. "Come in, come in. What brings you out here?"

"I came mostly to see you."

"Is anything wrong?"

"No, no. Well, not exactly." She untied the strings of her bonnet and removed it. "Can we talk?"

"Of course." Gesturing to the parlor, Cassandra stepped back. "I was just doing a little crocheting."

"What are you making?"

"Antimacassars for Zeb's upholstered chairs and the sofa. It's amazing how soiled the brocade gets when it's not covered properly."

"Oh, doillies. I've never heard them called that before."

"It refers to that new men's hairdressing from back east that gets all over the furniture. But enough about that. Sit down and tell me what's on your mind."

Emmeline looked around furtively, barely appreciating the elegant furnishings. "Are we alone?"

"Yes." Cassandra had begun to frown. "Are you sure nothing's wrong? You look distressed."

"I am. It's—it's hard to talk about."

"Then let's go into the kitchen. I'll make us a nice cup of tea and you can take all the time you need. Zeb never gets home until very late, especially when he stops at the boardinghouse for supper. This big house is going to waste, if you ask me, but that's neither here nor there."

Following Cassandra down the hallway and into the immense, country kitchen, Emmeline remarked, "Oh, my. This is twice the size of the ranch's kitchen. Do you take care of it all by yourself?"

"Yes, and if my brother was home more it would be a real chore, I tell you. I keep insisting he needs a full-time housekeeper, but he argues that he's not here enough for it to matter." She opened the firebox of the iron cookstove, threw some light wood onto the glowing embers and slammed the door. "There. We'll have hot water for tea in no time."

"I didn't come for a tea party," Emmeline said softly. "I came to get your advice. About men."

"Whoa!" The other young woman spun around, sloshing water out of the spout of the kettle she had started to fill. "Oops. You caught me by surprise."

"Sorry. I had a serious talk with my mother today. But even after what she told me, I don't know what I'm going to do."

Cassandra set the water on the stove, returned to

Emmeline and grasped her hands. "Let's start at the beginning. You aren't in a family way, are you?"

"Of course not!" She shook her head and gaped, astonished. "What a terrible thing to say."

"Simmer down," Cassandra said soothingly. "You were always insisting you hated the idea of marriage, so I just assumed something dreadful had happened. You know. Some man had attacked you and—"

"No, no. It's nothing like that. I just, well, I just wondered if you knew anything about being a proper wife."

"All right, that does it. What in the world makes you ask?"

"Maybe I shouldn't have come." Emmeline tried to pull free, but her friend held her hands tightly.

"Oh, no, you don't," Cassandra drawled, smiling. "You're not leaving here until you tell me why you're interested in learning about becoming a wife."

Tears misted Emmeline's vision as she answered, "Because, I'm afraid I've fallen in love."

Will had helped with framing the town hall all afternoon, then bid the other volunteers goodbye and headed home. The closer he rode to the Circle-L, the more apprehensive he grew.

Seeing Emmeline again was all he could think about, day and night, in spite of constant efforts to avoid her, to put her out of his mind. Clearly, that was an impossible goal. She was already so much a part of his every waking thought—and of his dreams—that he figured he may as well stop trying to focus on anything else.

Unsure of exactly what he was going to do, to say to her, he paused in the barn long enough to give his sorrel a rubdown and stable him for the night. Her family would be present during supper, as would his whole crew, so there was no way he'd be able to speak to her privately at that time. That was a relief, in a way, because it meant he'd have longer to form his ideas into sensible pleas—or to decide to keep silent.

Saying nothing was probably the wisest course, Will reasoned. After all, what did he have to offer Emmeline except a life of hard work and a tenuous future? Then again, if he included her whole family in his overall plans, she might look more favorably on his proposal that they have no children of their own. She was already helping to raise her siblings. Maybe that would be enough family for her, even if her mother saw to the younger children, as she was beginning to do.

Suppose it wasn't enough? he asked himself. What then? Would Emmeline understand his position or was he being unreasonably selfish? And if she did appear to agree, would it be an honest response or would she be pretending because she knew that was what he wanted to hear?

Taking a deep breath and squaring his shoulders, he dusted himself off and headed for the bunkhouse to spruce up before facing her. Yes, he was stalling. But the very notion of looking into Emmeline's beautiful blue eyes and pouring out his heart to her was more unsettling to him than having to stand unarmed and face a whole tribe of rampaging Indians.

That comparison was so vivid it made Will smile. He was still amused when he entered the kitchen later, fully expecting to encounter Emmeline.

To his chagrin, her mother and sister were the only ones present. Joanna was stirring a pot of beans and salt pork on the stove, and Bess was setting the long table. Both looked at him when he entered but neither smiled.

"Where's Emmeline?" Will asked.

Drying her hands on her apron, Joanna shrugged. "I thought you'd know. You were in town too, weren't you?"

"Yes. What does that have to do with Emmeline?"

Instead of answering, the older woman took a piece of paper out of her apron pocket and handed it to him.

As Will read, the reality of the situation plunked into the pit of his stomach and lay there like one of Hank's rock-hard biscuits.

"When did she leave?" Will asked.

"I don't know. I was napping with Glory. When I awoke and came looking for Emmeline, all I found was that note."

"Well, I didn't pass her or meet up with her on the road from town, so she must still be there," he said, scowling. "What was she thinking, making that trip alone?"

"It's not really that far," Joanna countered. "I'm sure she'll be back soon." She eyed the food on the stove. "She knows she's needed here."

Which is one more reason to worry, Will told himself. What could Emmeline have been thinking? She knew he would have gladly escorted her himself, or at least assigned one of his men to do so. Even in broad daylight the trip was fraught with hidden dangers. Worse, it would soon be nightfall. Why hadn't she come home?

"I'm going after her," Will announced. "If I'm not back by suppertime, send Clint after me."

Joanna was wringing her hands. "Do you think Emmeline may be in trouble?"

"If she isn't already, she will be when I find her," Will said firmly.

"Don't—don't hurt her. Please?" Joanna pled softly, plaintively.

That stopped Will in his tracks. He whirled, astounded and hurt. "If you think I'd lay a hand on her, or any other woman, then you're as far around the bend as she is."

The tears of relief in the older woman's eyes cut him to the quick.

Chapter Fifteen

By the time Emmeline had listened to Cassandra's repeated assurances that all men were not to be feared the way she had her father, the hour was late and the mercantile was closed for the day. Therefore, she couldn't stop to pick up her order.

Frustrated, she decided to stable the packhorse at Zeb's and head for home, then return the following morning for the supplies.

She hadn't intended to be away so long, but her conversation with Cassandra had been so enthralling and informative she'd lost track of the hour.

"Take care and go straight home," the other woman cautioned.

Emmeline gave her a farewell hug. "I will. Hopefully, I haven't been missed."

"Don't count on that. I know Will was with my brother earlier, but I imagine he's gone back to the ranch by now." She giggled. "And if he's there, you'd better believe he's looking for you."

"I hope you're right about that." Emmeline turned to go, knowing she was blushing. She led the mare up to the side of the porch and used its added height to gain the stirrup and mount without difficulty.

Cassandra stood back and waved a dainty, lace-edged handkerchief as Emmeline straightened her skirts to modestly cover her boot tops, then reined the horse and rode away.

She knew without a shadow of doubt that she'd been blessed to find such true friends and she had to attribute that directly to having been near High Plains when the wagon wreck had occurred. Just imagine. If that tornado had not overtaken them when and where it had, she might never have gotten to know any of the townspeople, especially not the one man who had captured her heart.

Thoughts of Will Logan brought a smile to her face and lightness to her spirit. Life was good, and getting better by the minute. As soon as she got back to the Circle-L, she'd find a way to *make* him discuss the future with her. If Cassandra was correct, the poor man had been suffering because he wasn't sure of her affection and she would be doing him a favor by speaking her mind.

As far as Emmeline was concerned, there was little chance that her wise friend had been wrong in her assessment of Will's feelings. Not only was it plausible that that was what had been bothering him of late, it was exactly what Emmeline had yearned to hear.

The setting sun bathed the prairie leaves and grasses in orange and crimson, making the clover, dogbane and milkweed look even more lovely, as if surrounded by halos of light. A mild breeze was blowing from the south, carrying with it the spicy scent of sage and the freshness of the balmy air.

Lulled into heedlessness by her pleasant musings and the beauty of the countryside, Emmeline rode along in dreamy silence and hummed a tune. She wasn't sure what she would say to Will or how she would begin, but she was going to force him to discuss their relationship, one way or another. Period.

Beneath her, the easy gait of the mare was suddenly interrupted. Its body tensed. Its muscles bunched an instant before it jumped back and sideways, nearly unseating her.

"Whoa!" She grabbed the saddle horn and held tight. The horse whinnied. It leaped. It bucked.

Emmeline screamed. Her toes slipped from one stirrup, then the other. Grasping with her knees, she fought to stay mounted. What in the world could have spooked the usually placid animal?

Her thoughts immediately answered, *Indians!* Eyes wide, she searched the tall grasses beside the trail as the horse stopped lunging and broke into a run. She couldn't spot any adversaries. Nor could she control the frightened mare.

Still grasping the saddle with one hand, she yanked back on the reins with her other. It was no use. The horse had taken the bit in its teeth and was running away with her. If she was fortunate enough to stay aboard the frightened little mare, the animal would probably tire and let her resume control eventually. For the present, all she could hope for was to keep from being pitched off onto the rocky ground.

"And to figure out where I end up," Emmeline added, clenching her teeth and trying to get her bearings.

They were racing across the prairie without benefit of trail or other familiar landmarks. Once the sun had set, she'd have little idea which way was home—or how long it would take her to get there, assuming she and the horse were in any shape to travel by then.

Her teeth jarred. Her arms ached with fatigue. She would not be able to hold on much longer.

Will's first stop was the mill where he was told that Zeb had gone to the boardinghouse to eat. He followed him to the two-story, whitewashed establishment and found him halfway through a meal of one of Rebecca Gundersen's tender steaks with all the fixings, as usual.

Zeb greeted him amiably. "Will! I thought you'd gone home. Pull up a chair and join me."

"I can't. Have you seen Emmeline?"

"Cassandra said she stopped by my house this afternoon and they had a nice long visit. Why?"

"She never got home."

Frowning, Zeb put down his fork. "Are you sure?"

"Positive. I took the same trail we always do. There was no sign of her."

Zeb threw his napkin onto the table and rose. "Then we'll form a search party. She can't have gone far." As the two strode to the door, he added, "Is it possible she accidentally took a wrong turn?"

"Unfortunately, yes," Will replied. "That woman could get lost walking from the house to the barn. She has absolutely no sense of direction."

"That's good news, then." He clapped his old friend on the back. "Come on. She's probably just gone astray."

"I hope so," Will said flatly, trying to control his escalating sense of foreboding. "I was planning to take your advice and ask her to marry me. At least I think I was."

"Then we'd sure better find her." Zeb grinned wryly at him. "Because I want to see the infamous bachelor Will Logan lassoed and harnessed by a good Christian woman."

"If she'll have me."

"Your chances will be better if you don't glower at her the way you are right now," Zeb warned. "I don't know her nearly as well as you do, but going by what my sister tells me, Miss Carter is not the type of woman to fold under pressure."

"I only hope she's strong enough to weather whatever the plains throws at her this time," Will said. "I can't lose her. Not now."

Emmeline was totally befuddled. She had managed to stay aboard the horse, even when it had stepped in a prairie-dog hole and nearly fallen, but that was of little help since the misstep had left the mare lame.

Now that the poor horse was over her initial fright, she was once again acting docile. Emmeline slid to the ground and kept hold of the reins while she examined the mare's injured pastern. It wasn't swollen yet, but chances were good it soon would be. Riding any horse when it was unsound was out of the question.

At this point in time, Emmeline saw only two options. She could either stay put with the limping mare and hope for rescue, or leave her behind and start walking.

If she'd had any notion of which way to head, she might have opted for the latter. Since she was unsure, she figured the best thing to do would be to remain right where she was. At least that way, the horse would be visible to anyone who came looking for them.

Then again, Emmeline realized belatedly, the grass had grown so tall in this part of the plains it was mostly above the animal's back and towered above her own head. If she'd been trying to hide, she couldn't have done a better job of it than this.

"Father, tell me what to do? Please? I don't want to cause my family undue worry and I don't know which way to go," she prayed, gazing at the heavens and hoping to locate the North Star. Clouds obscured most of the sky. Darkening, blowing, scudding clouds that she had not noticed before.

Was it going to storm again? She looked to the moon. It was not only in its waning phase, it was also haloed, which usually signaled an approaching storm. And it was rapidly being masked by thick clouds and mist rising from the ground as the temperatures dropped. Soon, she wouldn't be able to see ten feet in front of her, if that.

Near panic, Emmeline swiveled to assess her surroundings in more detail. To her left, the prairie seemed to rise, as if there were a hill there, although she couldn't be positive from where she stood. If she wanted to gain that high ground and keep the horse with her, she'd have to make the climb soon, before the path got any darker, and before the mare's foreleg got any worse.

"Come on, girl," she urged, giving the reins a tug. "We're going to walk just a little. You can do it. That's right. Good girl."

Watching the mare move stiffly, she was careful to keep from leading her too fast. The horse seemed to be doing pretty well, considering, but Emmeline didn't want to aggravate the injury and ruin the mare for keeps if she could help it.

Her reticule had been hooked to the saddle horn by its drawstrings. Now, she paused long enough to retrieve it and loop it around her wrist. The little gun was still stashed inside it and although she knew that such a weapon lacked much punch, she still felt better having it at hand.

Struggling to keep her long skirts and petticoats out of the tangled grass and brambles, she led the lame horse up the incline, continuing to urge it on with kind words and firm tugs.

"That's it, girl. You're doing fine. We're almost there," she said, mostly to hear her own voice and thereby help banish the unseen threats of the encroaching shadows.

Flint rocks slipped and skittered beneath their feet, making the last few yards the most treacherous.

Emmeline gained the highest point and found she could see for miles in the waning light. There were trees and grass and a few other knolls in view. There was not, however, a single sign of habitation.

The horse nickered and she reached to stroke its velvety nose. "I know your leg hurts, baby. And I'm really sorry. But it was your idea to go for a gallop, you know."

The mare nudged her hand as if asking for forgiveness. She sighed. There was nothing to be gained by getting mad at the horse. It had been frightened and had reacted predictably. It had fled without thought for the consequences.

Was there a lesson in that for her? she wondered. Perhaps. Perhaps she should have run as far and as fast from the Circle-L as possible instead of staying long enough to fall in love with its owner. Knowing what she knew now, would she do the same again?

"Oh, yes," she whispered into the silence of the night.

She was thinking about how much she cared for Will when she heard a rustling in the tall vegetation to her left. She froze. Listened. Then heard what sounded like the rattling of loose buttons inside a jelly jar.

Before she could react, the horse jerked the reins from her hand and reared on its hind legs, nearly toppling over on the uneven terrain.

Emmeline screamed. Her boot caught on a rock outcropping. She stumbled backward, lost her balance and landed in a heap. The bent grasses formed a nest around her as she fell, partially cushioning her landing, but it jarred her to the teeth just the same.

She raised her arms for protection, expecting to see the mare's front hooves descending to strike her.

Instead, she saw it recover its balance, wheel and race away in spite of its injury.

Emmeline's first thought was relief. Consternation quickly followed. And on the heels of that she started to imagine what Will's reaction would be when that mare came home without a rider. He had been very upset the last time she'd lost her mount, but that was probably nothing compared to how he was going to feel when he realized it had happened again.

Rising and dusting herself off, Emmeline appreciated the fact that she was unhurt. She might be embarrassed and flustered and mad at herself for getting caught in such a dilemma, but she was nevertheless thankful to be in one piece. It could have been much worse.

The noise of the buttons in the glass jar once again caught her attention.

Speaking of worse things...

She froze, afraid to move. That was a sound she'd heard enough times to identify it. Somewhere in the dark, very nearby, there lay a rattlesnake. And it was upset about having its territory invaded. By her.

Will, Zeb and a few other men fanned out from High Plains, each choosing his own trail. Will chose to follow the one he thought Emmeline would have taken, even though he'd seen no sign of her on his latest trip to and from town.

Part of him wanted to be angry at her while another part was so worried he could hardly think straight. The notion that he might have actually lost her forever kept nagging at the fringes of his mind, driving him frantic.

In the distance he heard a horse whinny. His sorrel tensed beneath him and snorted, anxious to pursue the sound. Will couldn't help remembering how he'd located Emmeline the last time they'd been separated on the prairie and he waited, almost expecting to see her horse appear once again. It did not. On the contrary, the calling appeared to be going away from him because it sounded fainter and fainter.

He supposed he could be hearing the horses of other members of the search party, but at this point he had no additional clue to Emmeline's possible whereabouts, so he figured he might as well leave the trail and follow that distant sound.

As he drew closer to a ridge that he knew eventually tied into the Oregon Trail, he began to notice more damage to the bluestem than one horse would have caused. Multiple riders or a small herd of bison had passed through here. Recently.

Dismounting, Will checked the ground. Horse tracks were thick. Only one of them was shod. That didn't mean the horse was the one that Emmeline had taken, or that it was now in the company of Indian ponies, but it sure looked as though that was the case.

Swinging into the saddle, Will slid his rifle out of its scabbard, checked to make sure it was loaded, then started to follow the trail the horses had left.

All he could think about was Emmeline. If he had to shoot to save her he would. Given the number of riders and the fact that he was alone, however, there was a good chance he'd be overpowered before he managed to free her. And then what would become of her?

For the first time since he'd learned of his mother's death, he felt tears filling his eyes. He steeled himself and blinked them away. He had a job to do. He must not weaken. Surely the Lord had not brought Emmeline into his life merely to snatch her away.

Praying silently and urging his horse through the tall grasses, Will kept his rifle at the ready and his eyes open. Even so, he was almost on top of the small party of Kansa braves before he spotted them.

They saw him, too. And they were leading a riderless, saddled horse that looked suspiciously like one from his string.

Having no choice, Will raised the arm holding his rifle to signal a greeting instead of aggression and slowly rode forward to face the Indians.

In the quiet of the deepening night, Emmeline's imagination ran rampant. Not only was she hearing the snake, she thought she heard other things, as well. Unidentified things. Frightening things.

If that rattler was not presently lurking beneath her petticoats and skirt, she should be safe enough.

Unless it decided to crawl under her hem, she added. That notion made her tremble so badly she nearly dropped her reticule.

The gun! Why hadn't she thought of that before? She might have only one shot in the chamber, but she had several more bullets with her. She could always reload. Providing she didn't fumble the little pistol and drop everything down where that snake lurked, she thought cynically. Her weapon of choice was a rifle, not an almost comical derringer. Such a gun might be all right for city folks and tinhorn gamblers, but it was next to useless way out here in the wild.

Nevertheless, she took it from her reticule and held it at the ready. The snake had grown suspiciously quiet. That was not a good sign. It meant he was on the move instead of remaining coiled, and there was no telling in which direction he might be headed.

She froze. Held her breath. Listened with every ounce of her being.

The grass rustled behind her.

She whirled, wide-eyed. The slim, lone figure of a Kansa brave was slowly rising to stand fully erect, but he was not looking at her. He was staring at a spot on the ground between them.

There was barely enough light by which to see the snake. She'd been right, it *was* on the move— but not to her. Unwinding like a thick rope, it was easing toward the Indian.

Raising her gaze for a brief moment, Emmeline

took in the fright in the young man's expression. He didn't look much older than Johnny and he was clearly unsure whether or not to move. As close as that rattler was to his legs and as large as it appeared to be, she knew it would have no trouble biting him from right where it lay.

She also realized that the Indian's presence there boded ill for her. He had not just happened to be passing when she'd found herself stranded. On the contrary, he had undoubtedly been sneaking up on her, and the only thing that had stopped him from attacking had been the unexpected presence of the snake.

Her hand wavered. She wouldn't have any trouble shooting the brave—or the rattler—at that distance no matter how puny her pistol was. The question was, which should be her target?

Considering the way her hand and arm were shaking, no matter which way she shot she figured she was only marginally assured of hitting what she'd aimed at.

Thoughts of turning to God for guidance were strong. He had brought her through many recent trials, so many that she no longer doubted His providence.

In the instant before she pulled the trigger, she managed a brief plea. "Lord, show me? Help me? I don't know what to do, but *You* do."

Comfort washed over her. She took aim and fired.

Chapter Sixteen

"That's my horse," Will said cordially as he rode up to the party of mounted braves. "Thanks for catching her for me."

Silence was his only reply.

The small group of Kansa were clad in blue and red breechcloth and wore deerskin leggings and moccasins. Their hair, which stood upright and remained only on the centerline of their scalps, was colored and stiffened with vermilion. One of them had his hair decorated with the tail feather of what Will assumed was an eagle and some wore necklaces of bear claws. Others had their ear cartilage pierced and festooned with porcelain or metal adornments as well as the kind of trinkets that Emmeline had encountered when she'd accidentally broken her attacker's necklace.

Will tried again. "Tell me where you found the

horse and I'll give her to you," he said. "A gift from the Circle-L to the brave Kansa warriors."

The feather-bedecked Indian laughed. "The horse is lame and we already have her. Why do we need your gift?"

"You sound like you went to a mission school," Will said, growing hopeful. "Was it the one that used to be in Council Grove?"

"Maybe."

"Then you should understand how I think. That horse means nothing to me. I just want to find its rider."

"The woman?"

Will gritted his teeth and calmed himself before answering. "Yes. My woman." He forced a smile. "She is troublesome, but I have grown used to her."

That brought laughter from many of the Indians, especially their spokesman. "All right." He pointed. "Back that way. We will ride with you so you don't get lost."

Will knew that was a feeble excuse, probably intended to hassle and intimidate him, but he didn't argue. As long as he located Emmeline, he'd gladly put up with as many taunts as they chose to dish out. Truth to tell, he was already surprised at their help-fulness. The Kansa had once been good-natured like this, but had hardened their hearts against the settlers lately, and little wonder, considering how poorly they had been treated, particularly by the federal government.

The Kansa who had been speaking urged his horse forward to ride abreast of Will. "I learned much at the mission," he said quietly. "They taught me to be a Christian. My son, too."

"Your people don't mind?"

"I worship the Great Spirit, just as they do. I call him Jesus."

"Ah, I see. Then you have no desire to kill me or my kin?"

The Kansa's laughter echoed in the quiet of the night. "I did not say that. Like you, I will do what I must to protect my brothers, my family."

"I understand," Will said. "In that respect we are not that different." He was about to go on, hoping to keep the Indian talking instead of giving him a chance to think about changing his mind, when a single shot echoed across the hills.

Will's horse startled and so did those of his companions.

Their pause was brief. He saw the Kansa reach for their weapons as he spurred the sorrel and raced with them across the plains, toward the area where they all assumed the shot had originated.

Thank the Lord Emmeline doesn't have a gun, Will thought. If she had, no telling what kind of mess she'd have gotten herself into.

* * *

Everything had happened too fast. Emmeline wasn't sure whether or not her bullet had found its intended mark.

The Indian screamed and threw himself backward to land, clutching his ankle.

A puff of dust from the impact of the bullet lingered around the scene, as if swept into the prairie air by an unseen broom.

The building wind carried the dust away in seconds and left a clear scene of havoc. Even now, she didn't know if her aim had been true. If she had missed, she might need another bullet, assuming she could see well enough to reload.

The Indian was writhing on the ground, but had ceased his cries. She hoped that was a good sign. And she also hoped he spoke English, because if he didn't and she had actually hit his leg instead of the rattler, she was going to have some tall explaining to do.

"Are you shot?" she asked, her voice tremulous.

He didn't answer. His dark eyes gleamed in the dimness. The clouds briefly opened for the moon and she could see a grimace on his youthful face.

"Did the snake bite you?"

"Ai."

"All right. I have another bullet. Where did it go?"

"Dead," he said.

"Are you sure?"

The Kansa stared at her as if she were as dumb as a prairie dog. Then he drew an arrow from his quiver and pointed with its tip. "There. Dead."

"Oh, thank the Lord," Emmeline said, meaning every word. "If you had landed on it and it was still able to bite, even from reflex, this could be much worse."

She knew she was babbling, but she was too relieved to keep silent. "I was afraid I'd shot you. That snake was really close to your feet."

"You shoot too slow."

"And you are very welcome," she said, trying to mute her cynicism. "How bad is the bite?"

Shrugging, the Indian began to unwrap the thongs that held his leather leggings and moccasins in place around his injured ankle.

Emmeline pocketed her gun and crouched nearby to get a better look at the wound. She'd seen settlers bitten right through their boots, so she was fairly certain the snake had sunk its fangs into the Indian's leg. The questions was, how much venom had it delivered and how long was the young man going to remain conscious before the poison took full effect?

"Do you have a knife?" she asked, not taking into account the fact that he might misinterpret her question.

He froze, staring at her.

"I put my gun away. See?" She displayed her empty hands, palms up. "I want to help you."

"Why?"

"Because it's the right thing to do," she said.

He grunted. "You Good Samaritan?"

"Yes! You know that Bible story?"

"From mission school," he said.

"Then you'll let me help?" She couldn't see his face except in shadow, but she sensed that he was starting to relax with her. That was a good sign. The weather, unfortunately, was rapidly worsening, tugging at her bonnet and skirts.

When the brave withdrew a large knife from a sheath on his belt, she almost jumped back.

There he sat, poised with the blade in his hand as if ready to plunge it into her heart, yet she remained stationary. Even injured as he was, the wiry young Indian could probably overtake and slay her if he wanted to, no matter how fast she ran. She would have to trust God for her deliverance.

She *was* fully trusting God again, she reaffirmed. After the wagon wreck she had questioned everything, including God's infinite wisdom, and that had weakened her faith. The peace and assurance she now felt in response to this particularly precarious situation eased her soul.

That was all the extra encouragement she needed. She extended her open hand once again.

The Kansa expertly flipped the knife, hesitated for mere moments, then slapped its hilt across her palm.

Bounding up the stony incline, Will's sorrel slipped because of its iron shoes. The Kansa horses were more sure-footed. Although he had been in the lead most of the way, they managed to pass him on the final leg of the climb.

He crested the ridge just in time to see one of the Indians lift a rifle and draw a bead on a crouched figure. It was hard to tell exactly what was transpiring, which was apparently the reason the brave was holding his fire.

The night was warm and the wind velocity was building from the south just as it had during the previous tornado.

Something moved along the ground. It lifted and rippled. A calico skirt! *Emmeline!*

Not knowing what else to do, Will spurred the sorrel hard and drove him against the mounted rider who was starting to lower and aim the rifle.

The horses clashed, shoulder to shoulder. The Kansa's gun went off, firing harmlessly into the air as he was knocked off balance.

The other braves immediately surrounded Will and he wondered if this was to be his last moment of life.

Then, from the ground, someone yelled, "Stop!"

"Who is that?" one of the braves shouted.

"Ish-tah-lesh-yeh."

The Indians scattered.

Will was summarily ignored. He dismounted barely in time to catch Emmeline as the Kansa pushed her up and away from their fallen comrade.

Will embraced her, scarcely believing either of them had come through such an ordeal without serious injury. "Are you all right?"

Clinging to him, Emmeline was trembling so much her voice quaked. "Yes, praise the Lord. There was a rattlesnake. I shot it, but I was too slow. It bit that boy before I got it."

Will held her at arm's length so he could see her face. "It didn't strike you?"

"No, I hit it, but—"

"With what? You don't have a gun."

"Yes, I do," she said softly. "Cassandra gave it to me."

"She *what?*" He fought to control his temper. "So *that's* where her pistol went."

"Don't blame her," Emmeline said. "She was just doing me a favor. I didn't want to go riding alone without some kind of protection."

"Why did you feel you had to go at all? I would have escorted you. You *know* that."

"Yes, but you were busy in town and…"

Will's gut was knotted, his heart still racing. Her pigheadedness had nearly cost her her life. And they were still not totally out of the woods. If those Indians got the wrong idea and decided she had been at fault for the snake's bite, they might have to make a run for it anyway. Doing that successfully was going to be next to impossible, particularly since they had only one horse.

Taking hold of her arm, he pushed her behind him so his body would shield hers. If his understanding of Kansa was correct, the one on the ground was called "Speckled Eye" in English. He wasn't familiar with that name of late, although he knew it had belonged to one of the old chiefs.

"How is he?" Will shouted to be heard over the ruckus and babbling among the Indians.

The Indian leader who had been to the mission school arose and approached. "The fangs went through his moccasins and out the other side. The poison is painful, but most was wasted. He will live."

"Then we'll be going," Will said.

"Take your other horse. It will be payment for the life of my son."

Emmeline peeked out past Will's shoulder. "Your son? I thought he looked awfully young. I have a brother about his age, I think."

"He is twelve summers."

Hearing that, Will figured he had a good idea what the boy was doing out there by himself. He was either on a vision quest or trying to earn the right to ride with the other men by stealing a horse and scaring a settler to death by hitting him to count coup. Only in this case, he'd come up against Emmeline Carter and she'd bested him. That was not a good thing for the youth's reputation, but it certainly pleased Will. If that snake had not been there…

He turned and mounted the sorrel, then reached down for Emmeline's hand, wrapping his fingers around her wrist and swinging her aboard behind him as they had done in the past. He didn't trust himself to say anything else at that moment for fear he'd chastise her too harshly. Not that she didn't deserve to be lectured.

She slipped her arms around his waist and hung on, pressing her cheek against his back. "That wind feels really ominous," she said loudly. "Aren't you troubled?"

Yes, but not about the weather, Will thought, holding his peace. He wasn't sure if he was more angry at Cassandra for giving Emmeline the gun or at Emmeline for thinking that tiny pistol was sufficient protection for riding across the plains and facing Indians.

Mulling it over as they headed for home, he decided it wasn't necessary to choose which woman was worse. He was equally furious with both of them.

"That boy was in such terrible pain. I hope he'll be all right," Emmeline remarked, hoping to coax Will into making conversation. He had said so little since they'd left the injured Indian, she was imagining all sorts of things, such as the likelihood that Will was mad at her. She supposed he had a right to be upset, although she had acted with the best of intentions.

She knew better than to admit why she had felt such a strong impulse to visit Cassandra by herself, especially when Will was acting out of sorts. Therefore, she fell back on her secondary reason for the trip to town.

"I had planned to stop at the mercantile and pick up some supplies on my way home," she said, "but I was too late leaving Mr. Garrison's house. The store was already closed. I stabled the packhorse in his barn and thought I'd go again tomorrow to finish up."

Still, Will remained stoic and didn't comment.

As far as she could tell, he was sulking. Well, fine. Let him brood. That didn't mean she had to ride the whole way back to the ranch in silence.

"I was touched by the way those Indians acted," she said, speaking past Will's shoulder. "The boy even had some Bible knowledge. He called me a Good Samaritan. Isn't that sweet?"

Waiting, she heard no reply. Will did, however, nudge the sorrel into a little faster walk. She assumed he'd be galloping if they hadn't had to take it easy for the sake of the limping mare they were leading.

"I think family is as important to them as it is to us, don't you? That Kansa father was just as nice as could be after he learned I'd helped his son. Children are so important."

Giggling softly, she stopped herself before foolishly adding what was in her heart, namely, that she yearned to be the mother of a big brood.

"Do you think so?" Will asked.

The fact that he had finally spoken took her by surprise and loosened her tongue. "Oh, yes. Children are everything. Mama says she doesn't know what she'd do without the four of us. She can't wait to become a grandmother."

She felt Will tense. Were his sensibilities offended by her foolish plain speaking? Possibly. Still, what was already said could not be taken back so she would just have to hope he wasn't too upset.

"Please forgive me," she added. "I certainly had no intention of making you uncomfortable. You've been an excellent benefactor and we are all much obliged."

"Understood. You and your family can all stay on the Circle-L as long as you want, even if the twins do turn up," Will said flatly. "I'd never make any of you leave."

Emmeline chewed on her lower lip as she pondered his words, his tone. He'd sounded more resigned than amiable, as if he was only making the offer because he felt beholden for some reason. She would much rather have heard him say he *wanted* her to stay on.

She sighed and pressed her cheek to his back as

they rode. The wind was cutting through her clothing, but that wasn't the only reason she felt cold all of a sudden. Will's evident indifference had given her the chills all the way to the marrow of her bones.

And, adding insult to injury, it was beginning to rain. She cuddled closer.

"I don't suppose you brought a slicker," he remarked.

"No. Did you?"

"I left in kind of a hurry," he said, and she could tell he was not feeling the least bit charitable.

"I am sorry I caused you worry," Emmeline told him. "I didn't dream I'd be this late getting home. And I did leave a note."

"I know. Your mother showed it to me."

"Then you already know I meant no harm."

"What you meant and what actually occurred are worlds apart, madam. Pull a crazy stunt like that again and I may just leave you out there to fend for yourself."

"You don't mean that."

She heard him make a derogatory noise under his breath before he finally said, "No. I suppose I don't."

Chapter Seventeen

Because of stormy weather and muddy, rutted roads, it was several days after their encounter with the Kansa before Will had been able to send Clint into town as an escort for Emmeline, her sisters and their mother while they all shopped.

Will figured it was sensible to get them out of the house at once so he could have some peace; some quiet time in which to think through his dilemma.

It had already become clear to him that allowing Emmeline to remain at the Circle-L without inadvertently showing his disappointment regarding their future was going to be impossible. In retrospect, he supposed he'd been an idiot to assure her that her family could continue to live there, but at the time it had seemed best.

Now that the threat of danger was past and he'd settled down, however, he could see that their current, day-by-day arrangement wasn't going to work. At least not for him.

He was mulling over the notion of building himself another house and abandoning the existing one to the Carters, when he rounded the corner of the barn and nearly collided with Hank.

"Oh, good," the older man said, his ruddy cheeks flushing even more than usual. "I was comin' to look for you, boss. I need to ask you something."

"Sure. Come on. I've got a couple of heifers penned up out back that I want to check on."

"I just looked at 'em. They're fine."

As overwrought as he was already, Will wasn't in the mood for any of Hank's complaints, so he sought to shorten their conversation. "Okay. Ask away. Just don't expect a raise till the fall roundup. I'm a tad short of extra money right now."

"Because of the widow woman and her kids, right?"

"That's part of it." Folding his arms across his chest, Will leaned back against the side of the barn and frowned. "How I manage this place is really none of your concern."

"It might be," Hank said, more tentative than Will had ever heard him before.

"Well then, spit it out, man. Speak your piece. I haven't got all day."

"You see now? That's part of the reason I ain't been in no hurry to bring this up. You're soundin' more like I used to every day, and I gotta tell you, Mr. Logan, it ain't good. No sirree. You used to be a real easygoing fella, before them settlers moved in, and I was thinkin' I'd take a few of 'em off your hands, so to speak."

That statement stiffened Will's spine and caused him to scowl. "What are you talking about? I told you I needed you as a cowhand, not a cook, so don't go getting any ideas about changing back to the way things used to be."

The old man shook his head. "No, no. It ain't like that. I was just thinkin', I mean if I…" He cursed under his breath. "Aw…"

Seeing Hank tongue-tied was so unusual it made Will smile in spite of his dour mood. "Whatever it is, just say it. I can take it."

"Okay. I been thinkin' I might ask the widow Carter to be my wife."

Will almost laughed till he realized that the old man was serious. "You? Marry? Why now?"

"Why not?" Hank said. "I ain't gettin' any younger and she needs somebody to look after her and them young'uns. Might as well be me, that is, if you could see your way clear to let us build a little cabin out here. I know Miz Carter'd want to stay by her oldest girl."

"She'd have to live with you, too," Will blurted. "It would ruin Emmeline's reputation if the rest of her family moved out of the house and she stayed. She'd never find a good husband."

"Ain't you gonna ask her to marry you? I thought sure you was. The way you two been makin' calf's eyes at each other, that's what everybody figured would happen."

"Well, it's not, so forget it."

"What about me and the widow woman?"

Will had to subdue the urge to mutter in a self-deprecating manner. "How should I know? I suppose you should talk to *her* about it instead of me." He shrugged and pushed away from the wall where he'd been leaning. "Mrs. Carter is already using the only bedroom. If she agrees to marry you, you may as well move into the house with her. Their wagon will be repaired soon and some of the children can bunk in that, temporarily, if you want more privacy."

"That's right nice of ya, Mr. Logan. I'm beholden."

"Yep. That's me," Will said with a sigh. "I'm such a great man I've talked myself out of house and home."

"You could change your mind and speak to Miss Emmeline. I'm pretty sure she'd be interested."

"No," Will barked, angry at himself most of all. "She hankers after a big family and that's not for me."

"Youngsters are a lot of help on a ranch like this," Hank reminded him.

"If they have a decent father, maybe. If not, they end up soured on life and hating everybody."

"Am I supposed to think that's how you feel?"

the old man asked. "'Cause if I am, I gotta say I don't agree. Up till recently you've been a right fine gentleman and a good boss. There's no good reason for you to speak ill of yourself. That boy Johnny, he thinks the world of you. And the little one does, too. She's always jabberin' on about how she cottons to *Mr. Will*."

"It's not up for discussion," Will insisted. "I've made up my mind and since you seem to have, too, I suggest you propose to Mrs. Carter as soon as she returns from town. I assume she'll feel she needs to stay in mourning for a while yet, but since you're no spring chicken, maybe she'll agree to marry soon."

"I hope so," Hank said, blushing. "I ain't been able to think of much else since she showed up out here."

Welcome to the club, Will thought, disgusted. He was just as bad in regard to Emmeline. Maybe worse. At least Hank was in a position to do something about his feelings for the woman of his choice. He, on the other hand, was bound by his conscience to say nothing. Do nothing.

If he could have believed for one second that he'd be able to put his love for Emmeline out of his mind and heart he'd have done so immediately. The very thought of trying to left him sweating and feeling as low and lifeless as a buffalo wallow.

The way Will saw his dilemma, he was either going to have to build another house for himself on the portion of his ranch that lay on the far side of the river, or force Hank to leave and take the whole family away with him. Given the way their current arrangement was working for everyone but the owner of the Circle-L, namely him, he figured he was the logical one to vacate.

In a way, Hank had been right about him. He did exhibit compassion for others, too much in this case. Because he loved Emmeline so deeply he was willing to make any sacrifice to keep her happy and to properly care for her family, even if that meant that he'd have to literally give away his home.

Normally, a trip to town with her family would have thrilled Emmeline. This time, however, she made it with trepidation.

Will had scarcely spoken to her since he had rescued her from the Indians and she wasn't sure how to take his silence. She'd assumed, at first, that he was simply upset about her venturing out alone. Now that she'd had time to think about it, she was sure there was more involved. He was avoiding her. Period. He'd turned and walked the other way more than once, rather than face her. She was positive she was not imagining his actions or giving them more weight than they deserved. The man's moodiness was starting to remind her of her own father and that comparison gave her the shivers. She hadn't seen him raise his voice or his hand to anyone yet, but was it only a matter of time?

Leaving her mother and sisters to their own devices once they arrived back at home, Emmeline laid aside the brown-paper-wrapped package of lilac-printed cotton fabric she'd bought at Johnson's mercantile and plunked down on the edge of the bed to stare out the window and muse.

To her delight—and despair—Will Logan was grooming a horse outside the barn. The sight of him thrilled her. She didn't know exactly when his mere presence had begun to affect her so, but looking at him was as pleasurable as viewing a summer sky and basking in the warmth of the sun.

Even when he was grumpy or avoiding her, as he had been, she yearned for a glimpse of him. And the sound of his voice never failed to send delightful shivers up her spine.

Emmeline leaned forward, rested her elbows on the windowsill, cupped her chin in her hands and watched him curry the sorrel. His movements were steady, strong, assured. She wished she felt half that confident about the way he'd been behaving of late. Surely he couldn't have changed his mind about caring for her. Not if Cassandra had been right.

Judging by the way Will had embraced her and held so tightly, he had been overjoyed when he'd found her safe and sound among the Indians on the prairie.

And after that? She wasn't sure what had happened. His disposition seemed to have changed the moment he'd found out she'd been armed, yet that wasn't a good enough reason for him to stay angry. If anything, he should have taken his bad temper out on Cassandra. After all, she had been the one to provide the little pistol. And besides, if she hadn't been armed, the situation could have turned much uglier.

As Emmeline continued to view the scene, Glory left the house and skipped across the yard toward Will. He paused in his labors, smiled and bent to speak with the child as she showed him something. It looked as if Glory was offering to share her newly purchased penny candy with the rancher.

Will smiled, held out his hand and accepted the gift, then carefully broke it in half and gave a portion back to the little girl.

She accepted it in her pudgy fingers. Standing on tiptoe, she leaned closer and placed a quick kiss on Will's cheek before turning and running back to the house. There was a wide grin on Glory's cherubic face, a smile that lit up the yard the way the sun warmed the open prairie.

Will's actions had been so kind, so gentle, they had brought tears to Emmeline's eyes. Many men, probably most, would have brushed off the little girl's generous gift the way a horse swished away a pesky fly with its tail. Will had not only accepted the overture, he had considered the child's feelings enough to break the candy in two and share it with its giver.

In addition, she realized with a start, his bad mood had not been visited on the innocent child the way Papa's always used to be. That was her answer, as surely as if she had heard a booming voice from heaven say, "This is a good man, a man you can trust."

She was about to turn away from the window when she saw Will stand, swipe at his own eyes, then go back to brushing the horse.

Emmeline was thunderstruck. Was he weeping? *No.* That couldn't be. Glory was a sweet child, yes, but offering him a little piece of her penny candy hardly called for such a powerful emotional reaction.

As she continued to observe him, however, Will paused, took out a hanky and blew his nose. It wasn't her imagination. Something had touched him enough to make him actually weep. The urge to run to him, to embrace him, to assure him that he was loved, was so strong it nearly caused Emmeline to sob out loud. Instead, she pressed her fingertips to her lips and took a shaky breath.

Should she follow the urgings of her heart and approach him when he was still so deeply moved? Would that embarrass Will or was it exactly what he needed? She hadn't the slightest idea.

Only one thing was clear, the man she loved with all her heart and soul was weeping because of the simple kindness of a child, and if there was some way to comfort him, she must do so.

With her mind made up and tears silently streaming down her cheeks, Emmeline whirled and headed for the barn.

Will saw her coming and strove to hide his damp eyes by concentrating on the horse's coat and keeping his back to her.

"I saw Glory give you some candy," Emmeline said, blotting her cheeks with her apron. "She's such a sweet child. Of course, she didn't offer to share with anyone else, me included."

"Yeah, well, she was sure sticky," Will grumbled.

"I don't doubt it. I can still smell the peppermint, even now."

Because he could sense that she was standing there watching him, he refused to turn. Maybe, if he pretended he was too busy to talk, she'd go away and he wouldn't have to explain why he'd disgraced himself by getting teary-eyed over a stupid piece of candy. It wasn't because of the candy, of course. He knew that. He also knew that both Glory and Johnny seemed to like him a lot, to look up to him. *Why?* was the unanswerable question. Why him? Was he truly good with children in spite of his upbringing? It was that possibility that had driven him to tears.

His senses were immeasurably heightened an instant before Emmeline's hand came to rest lightly on his forearm. Even through his shirtsleeve he could feel the warmth, sense the tenderness and concern emanating from her. She must have seen too much, must already know that the child's overture had touched him deeply. That was appalling. What must she be thinking?

Will sniffled rather than get out his handkerchief. "My allergies are really bad this time of year."

"Whatever you say." Emmeline continued to stand very close to him, so close that he was forced to look at her.

"Did you want something?" Will asked.

She nodded. "Yes. I need to speak with you."

"Maybe after supper," he said, trying to sound nonchalant and realizing that he'd failed miserably.

"No. Right now," Emmeline insisted. "If you need to go ahead and work on that horse, I'll help you. But we are going to get this settled between us."

"There's nothing to settle," Will said flatly, still fighting his feelings. "There is nothing between us."

"I had thought—had hoped—that there was, or could be," she told him.

Sensing a tremor in her voice, he looked up. The pathos on her lovely face cut him to the quick. She had never before looked that emotionally affected, not even after the tornado or at her father's funeral.

Without pausing to consider the possible ramifications of his actions, Will listened to his heart. He dropped the brush and opened his arms to her.

As Emmeline stepped into his waiting embrace, he caught a glimpse of tears sliding down her cheeks. He had done this to her. To both of them. He and his unacceptable background, his surety that he would never be a decent father. There was only one thing to do at this juncture. He was bound by honor to explain himself. There would never be a better time to do so.

Laying her cheek on Will's chest, Emmeline tried to keep from weeping, but to no avail. Her heart was breaking and she was at the end of her tolerance. Something had to give and apparently her self-control was what was about to snap.

"I, I don't mean to make you uncomfortable," she said haltingly. "I just—I just want to understand why you've grown so distant. I'm sorry I took the gun and rode out by myself and—"

He interrupted by cupping her damp cheeks and raising her face to his. "The problem is not your behavior," he said. "It's me. I could see that we were getting too serious and I chose to step back, that's all."

"Too serious for what?" she asked, blinking as she stared into his eyes. "I thought you cared for me."

"I do." Will shuddered. "That's the whole point. You deserve someone who can give you children and I can't."

"Children?" The answer suddenly came to her. "You've been avoiding me because I mentioned Mama wanting to have grandchildren? That's a ridiculous reason."

"Not to me it isn't. I know I'd make a lousy father. Ask Zeb. He'll tell you how badly my dad and grandpa used to behave."

"What does that have to do with you? Or with me?"

"Everything," Will said. "I was going to ask you to marry me before I realized how unfair that would be to you."

"Suppose you let me decide."

"There's nothing to decide. Circumstances have done that for us. In case you don't already know it, Hank is fixing to ask your mother to be his bride and I assume she'll accept. Once they're married, they'll need a place of their own. I've told Hank they can take over the main house."

"But, where will you and I live?"

"Haven't you heard a thing I've said? You can stay with your family. I'll move somewhere else. There's a good site on high ground across the river. I'll put up a new cabin out there so I won't be underfoot all the time."

She sighed, realizing that he was still not seeing her point. Apparently, beating around the bush didn't work with someone so literal minded.

Keeping her arms loosely around Will's waist, she gazed up at him and began to grin. "Look, cowboy, it's this way. You love me and I love you. Don't even try to run away or deny it."

"You'll get over me, once I'm not around."

"I doubt that," Emmeline said with conviction

and obvious devotion. "Because wherever you go, I'm going. If you stay here, then I'll stay too. If you move across the river, count on my showing up on your doorstep and making myself at home."

"You'll soil your reputation. I can't allow that."

"Then I guess you'll have to marry me and make an honest woman of me." She continued to look into his eyes, into his heart, until she saw a glimmer of hope.

"What about children? A family? Will you be satisfied to raise Glory and your siblings instead of having more babies?"

Blushing, Emmeline nevertheless refused to look away. She couldn't tell if Will meant he was unable to become a father or merely unwilling, and she was too shy to ask him to clarify. It didn't matter. Not really. Not if she was totally trusting God.

"Let's leave children up to the good Lord, shall we? I imagine He has His own plans for us. After all, we never should have met in the first place, yet here we stand."

"You don't know me."

"I know all I need to."

Will shook his head slowly. "No, you don't. My father and his father before him were cruel men."

So *that* was what was bothering him. Her heart rejoiced in finally knowing what to say, how to help him. She smiled. "What does that have to do with *you?*"

"Everything. It's in my blood."

"No." She shook her head while looking directly into his kindly eyes and willing him to believe her. "You're not like that. Not one bit. I've watched how you act around Johnny and he's the most difficult boy I've ever laid eyes on. Your simple tact and fairness have already helped him so much that I truly believe he'll grow up to be a fine man, and I couldn't have said that before we met you."

"I have tried to teach him to think before he acts and to be considerate of others."

"Yes, and he's much better for it."

"He has shown improvement, hasn't he?"

"Absolutely. And as far as Glory is concerned, she thinks the sun rises and sets with you. You should hear how she goes on and on about Mr. Will and how much she loves living on this ranch."

"Really?"

"I wouldn't be saying it if I wasn't convinced. You sell yourself short, Will. You're a fine, upstanding man and I will be proud to become your wife."

Cupping her cheeks, Will leaned closer and gave her a brief, gentle kiss before whispering, "Thank you."

That was nowhere near enough for Emmeline. She raised on tiptoe and returned his kiss with a fervor she hadn't dreamed was possible. She might have continued to cling to him and express her undying love, had Hank and Joanna not appeared on the back porch.

Emmeline giggled and eased out of Will's arms when she heard the old man give a raucous hoot and start to chuckle.

"Wanna make it a double weddin', boss?" he called.

"What do you say, Miss Emmeline? Will you marry me?"

"I thought you'd never ask," she replied, so happy she couldn't stop grinning. "I just bought some yard goods in lilac. How does that sound for a wedding dress?"

To her relief and delight, Will was smiling and gazing at her with undisguised affection. "That depends," he drawled. "How fast can you sew?"

She giggled. "How fast can you build us a cabin?"

Chapter Eighteen

Joanna and Hank had opted for a simple, private ceremony at home and had already been married for a week by the time Will and Emmeline tied the knot.

Had the town hall been intact, Will would have preferred to use that, rather than the cavernous community church. Someday, Lord willing, they'd have enough of a congregation to fill it, but so far that building was way too large and imposing for his taste.

Light streamed through the tall windows on either side, bathing the center aisle while Susannah Preston, the reverend's wife, banged away on a tinny piano that didn't sound melodious no matter who played it.

The rear and side doors had been left open to cool the place, but it was still summer in Kansas and thus warmer than was comfortable, especially since Will was wearing one of Zeb's fancy brocade vests under the dark wool suit his friend had insisted he also borrow.

By the time Zeb and Cassandra had gotten through outfitting him according to their standards, Will had felt so formal he'd almost shucked the whole suit in favor of his usual work clothes. He had kept his own boots, at least, although Cassandra had polished them till she could practically see her reflection in the leather.

Will fidgeted as he stood at the altar and waited. He had hired a buggy from Pete and assigned Clint to drive the bride and her kin into town. Now, he wished he'd done it himself. At least that way he'd know she was safe and well cared for.

He saw a flutter of excitement at the door. Susannah launched into a kind of march music that was even less easy on the ears than her previous piece had been.

Cassandra swept gracefully through the door and started down the aisle, but Will had eyes for only one woman. And there she was! His breath caught and a lump formed in his throat. He'd never seen a more beautiful sight in all his twenty-five years.

Emmeline's lilac dress made her look like an emissary of spring on the pristine prairie. She carried a bouquet of crown vetch, elderberry blossoms and prairie clover that Will had picked just for her. It was held together by pale purple silk ribbons from the mercantile, and more of those ribbons festooned her upswept hair.

The whole town had turned out for the festivities, including the ubiquitous Matilda Johnson, her daughter, Abigail, and husband Abe.

Percival Walker and Cassandra Garrison had made a handsome couple when they'd arrived, he in his tailored suit and she in that new, Paris-style hat, decorated with lace, feathers and mauve, velvet roses around the crown. Her matching suit was velvet, too, and she looked very elegant as the maid of honor, but everyone's attention was focused mostly on the bride. Especially Will's.

Hank, Emmeline's new stepfather, thinning hair slicked back, shirt pressed and braces in place, escorted her down the aisle and beamed with pride.

Off to the side, Joanna wept while Bess looked around at the church and seemed to be actually observing more than was her usual practice, *Praise the Lord.*

Glory started to jump up and down as soon as she spied Emmeline, clapping her hands until her mother leaned down and shushed her.

Johnny stood beside Will and held the delicate ring Will had had made, set with diamonds from the brooch his mother had given him as her parting gift, all those years ago.

When he had shown it to Emmeline to get her approval, he'd explained its origin. "My mother's brooch provided the diamonds. The jeweler in Manhattan had to send to Saint Louis for the mounting. I hope that's okay with you."

"It's lovely. I'm sure no bride has ever been given a more precious ring. I'll cherish it always."

"Then why are you crying?"

She had grinned at him and made him smile when she'd said, "I always cry at weddings and I thought I'd get a head start this time."

Will's choice of Johnny as best man had been a calculated one. He knew Zeb would understand. He didn't need the boy's help but figured it was prudent to include him if possible and to his surprise, the young man had taken to the job, clearly thrilled to have been asked. That kid really had made progress. The best part was that Emmeline was still giving much of the credit for her brother's reformation to Will.

She was right about a lot of things, that included, he mused, holding out his hand to her as she drew near. Maybe she was right about him and children, too. He certainly had taken to her brother and little sister without any difficulty. And they, to him.

As Emmeline placed her hand in his, Will had to fight back tears for the second time in as many weeks. This woman, this extraordinary, beautiful, wise woman, was about to become his wife. If anyone had told him a few months ago that he would be standing at the altar, about to take sacred vows to spend the rest of his life with a woman he adored, he would have laughed. Yet, here they were.

Smiling at his bride, he turned to Reverend Preston, with Emmeline beside him, and the service began.

"Dearly beloved, we are gathered…"

As they left the sanctuary half an hour later, the sun was beaming into the churchyard as if bestowing its own blessing on their union.

They stood on the porch, arm in arm. Emmeline couldn't stop grinning so widely that her cheeks hurt. Even Bess's continuing muteness and thoughts of the missing twins were not enough to steal her joy. Wonder of wonders, she was now Mrs. Will Logan and would soon become the mistress of the second house built on the Circle-L, thanks to the combined efforts of many of Will's friends from town. If she had not seen the little cabin going up she would not have believed it could have been constructed so quickly.

Scores of well-wishers flanked the path leading from the front doors. Scanning the crowd and recognizing more people than she'd thought she would, Emmeline was pleased to note that many of the women of High Plains seemed happy for her in spite of the fact that she had "stolen" one of their most eligible bachelors.

The only really disappointed expressions in the group belonged to some mothers and their young, unmarried daughters, such as Matilda Johnson and her Abigail, and Mrs. Morrow, the dressmaker, and her shy Winifred.

To Emmeline's surprise and delight, Winifred had magnanimously offered to help her complete her wedding dress and she had let the girl work the tiny buttonholes in the fitted bodice when it had seemed the Carter women were going to have trouble finishing in time. In the process, she had gotten to know the young woman better and genuinely liked her.

Pausing on the top step, Emmeline held up her wildflower bouquet and made ready to throw it, hoping that Winifred would not be too bashful to reach out or be pushed aside by other, more eager, single ladies.

She drew her arm back and launched the bunch of flowers in a high arc, sorry to see it snatched from Winifred's grasp by the claws of Abigail Johnson, who then displayed it as if she had just won the most coveted prize in the territories.

As far as Emmeline was concerned, the only real prize was the handsome man at her side and that apt comparison made her smile wistfully and gaze at him. The ring Will had placed on her finger was not only a token of his undying love, it was also a lasting symbol of his mother's love for him, making it even more precious.

Raucous shouting at the rear of the crowd drew Emmeline's attention. Apparently, the Tully brothers were up to their old tricks, causing a commotion as usual. They were slapping each other on the back, hooting and pointing at a blond young woman as if she were a laughingstock.

Emmeline tugged on Will's arm. "See those three disgusting men? I hope they don't start a fight and spoil things. They were a terrible influence when they were part of our wagon train."

"They've been troublesome here in High Plains, too. Don't worry. Edward Gunderson's back there with his sister and Pete's probably not far off. They can handle the situation."

"Are you sure? I know blacksmiths are strong, but those Tully brothers are big and nasty. Who are they harassing?"

"Looks like Rebecca Gundersen."

"The Norwegian cook for the boardinghouse? I don't believe I've met her yet."

"You will. I'm planning to take you there for supper. Can't have my bride slaving over a hot stove on her wedding day."

"I don't mind. It will be my pleasure to fix meals for you, especially in my new kitchen." She felt her cheeks warming. "For the rest of my life."

"Starting tomorrow," Will said. "I've invited the rest of your family to join us for supper, too. Why don't we walk over there instead of taking the buggy I rented. It's not far."

Emmeline slipped her hand farther through the

crook of her husband's elbow, pulled him closer and smiled dreamily. "I would love to walk out with you, Mr. Logan, but what will everyone say?"

"That Mr. and Mrs. Logan are a mighty handsome couple," he answered, grinning.

Emmeline silently agreed. Thinking of herself as married was a strange, wonderful sensation. She just hoped she was up to the task of being a good wife. Parts of her upcoming duties still gave her pause, yet she dearly loved the man at her side and was determined to work hard to please him.

Blushing, she tried to imagine their first night together and failed. Cassandra had told her some things to expect, of course, as had her mother. Beyond that, she would trust Will. He would never hurt her. That was all she needed to know.

Proceeding through the throng, Emmeline noted that the Tullys had edged closer to their projected path and were now between them and the main road leading to Mrs. Jennings's boardinghouse. That was not good. Not good at all.

She tightened her hold. "Let's go around. I don't want to face those horrid men."

"Nonsense. They're the outsiders in High Plains. We're among friends."

"Still…"

He patted her hand. "Come on. I want you to meet Rebecca, anyway. She's fairly new here, too, and I know she could use a friend like you."

"All right. Whatever you say."

The closer they drew to the young, blond woman, the louder the Tullys' voices grew. They were clearly taunting the boardinghouse cook, and their insinuations made Emmeline blush. She couldn't tell exactly what they were talking about, but it sounded as if they were accusing Rebecca of improper behavior.

As Emmeline watched, the cook gathered her apron in her hands, pressed it over her mouth, turned and fled.

Left behind, the Tullys laughed raucously, their gruff ways attracting far too much attention to suit Emmeline. Whatever they had said was probably an outright lie meant to cause anguish or stir up trouble, or both. Of all the people she had met since leaving Missouri, those three were by far the most odious. She'd rather encounter a dozen wild Indians than any one of those brothers.

As Will escorted her past Abe and Matilda Johnson, Emmeline tried to coax a smile from the woman and was greeted with a raised chin and a sniff of disdain, instead.

That didn't matter, Emmeline assured herself. As long as she had Will and the rest of her loving family, social acceptance from the town's ladies or their ilk was unnecessary.

"I hope poor Rebecca is going to be all right," Emmeline said aside to Will. "She looked really upset."

"She'll be fine. I saw her brother, Edward, follow her, and Pete Benjamin's not far behind. They'll make sure she's okay."

"I know how hard it is to feel a part of this place, even now, so it must be really hard to come to a foreign country and try to fit in."

Will smiled and covered her hand again. "See? I told you you'd be a perfect friend for her. Cassandra has tried to help her adjust, too, but there will always be those who have trouble accepting strangers."

"Thankfully, you're not one of them."

Behind her, she heard Mrs. Johnson's "Hmmph" and assumed it was because she had spoken to Will so intimately in public.

Well, too bad. She loved her husband more than she had ever imagined one person could love another and she was not about to pretend they weren't enamored of each other. Let folks say what they would. She was now the happiest person on the plains and she was not about to deny her joy for the sake of overblown propriety.

Each step she took beside Will was another that led to their future, their destiny, Emmeline mused. There would be problems, but they would overcome them. Together.

This wasn't the end.

It was just the beginning.

* * * * *

Dear Reader,

When I said, at the end of this book that this was just the beginning, I meant it in several ways. It was the beginning of a new life for Emmeline and Will, yes, but it was also not the end of the tales of High Plains, Kansas. The next book in this series is *Heartland Wedding* by Renee Ryan, and the third and last is *Kansas Courtship* by Victoria Bylin. By then, you'll know all our secrets and the answers to your questions, I promise.

As you may know, I wrote the first book in the contemporary series, too. Stepping back in time and visualizing the same kind of disaster in 1860 was an interesting and challenging task. Believe me, it's comforting to know that I have a real storm shelter right out my back door, because we do get twisters around here, particularly in the spring. I trust God, but I also believe He expects me to make use of the brains He gave me and head for the cellar when I need to!

I love to hear from readers. The quickest replies are by email, Val@ValerieHansen.com or check out my Web site, www.ValerieHansen.com. By regular mail you can reach me at P.O. Box 13, Glencoe, AR 72539

Blessings,

Valerie Hansen

QUESTIONS FOR DISCUSSION

1. Have you ever imagined yourself living in another time, such as the 1800s? Did you think it would be fun, or hard to do?

2. Can you see yourself coping with the rigors of pioneer life, particularly while traveling with a wagon train?

3. Have you ever been frightened by a storm? When and where?

4. When you see photos or read stories of being overtaken by a tornado, can you see yourself in such a dilemma? What would you do?

5. When Emmeline sent Bess and the twins away to seek shelter, was she being sensible? Could that have been the best choice, under those circumstances?

6. Meeting Will in the mercantile was very advantageous for the Carter family. What might they have done without Will's help?

7. In 1860, there was much unrest in the territories and even more in Missouri. I didn't have room to deal with the border skirmishes and the

clash of ideology, but it is good to keep in mind that war was looming.

8. Since there was a good chance of war, does it seem odd that the pioneers in High Plains were more concerned with their current, day-to-day problems? Why was that normal?

9. The society dynamics of the small town were what formed many personal opinions, right or wrong. Have you ever lived in a little town where everyone knew everyone else's business? Was it difficult to cope?

10. When Emmeline's mother is left widowed, is it logical that she would seek to remarry, even though her late husband had been abusive? Why or why not?

11. Emmeline needs a job. Why did she ask Cassandra such specific questions about possible employment? Were there other choices she didn't mention? Why might she have omitted them?

12. At thirteen, is Johnny old enough to be gainfully employed and help the family? Remember, this is 1860. Do you think today's children or youth would be capable of carrying the burdens these settlers' children did?

13. Buffalo roam the flint hills freely and there are no fences to contain the cattle, either. When barbed wire came into use, was it part of the reason that the wild herds died out?

14. The High Plains Community Church is too big for the town as it stands at the time of this story. Why would people build such a large edifice? Did you know that missionary societies and others back East often financed such projects?

15. The Indian school in Council Grove has come and gone by 1860. Why do you suppose it failed? Why would the Kansa and other Indians send their children there in the first place? (In my research, I found that many of the young boys who were sent to live at the school were orphans whose parents had either been killed or had died from disease.)

16. When Emmeline and Will marry, her wedding dress is not white. Was that common back then? Why? Could it be because clothing was so hard to come by and a gingham or calico dress could be worn long after that one special day?

*Scandal surrounds Rebecca Gunderson after
she shares a storm cellar during a deadly
tornado with Pete Benjamin.
No one believes the time she spent with him
was totally innocent.
Can Pete protect her reputation?*

*Read on for a sneak peek of
HEARTLAND WEDDING by Renee Ryan,
Book 2 in the AFTER THE STORM:
THE FOUNDING YEARS series
available February 2010
from Love Inspired Historical.*

"Marry me," Pete demanded, realizing his mistake as the words left his mouth. He hadn't asked her. He'd told her.

He tried to rectify his insensitive act but Rebecca was already speaking over him. "Why are you willing to spend the rest of your life married to a woman you hardly know?"

"Because it's the right thing to do," he said.

Angling her head, she caught her bottom lip between her teeth and then did something utterly remarkable. She smoothed her fingertips across his forehead. "As sweet as I think your gesture is, you don't have to save me."

A pleasant warmth settled over him at her touch, leaving him oddly disoriented. "Yes, I do."

She dropped her hand to her side. "I don't mind what others say about me. You and I, *we,* know the truth."

Pete caught her hand in his, and turned it over in his palm. "I told Matilda Johnson we were getting married."

She snatched her hand free. "You…you…*what?*"

He spoke more slowly this time. "I told her we were getting married."

She did *not* like his answer. That much was made clear by her scowl. "You shouldn't have done that."

"She was blaming you for luring me into my own storm cellar."

The color leached out of Rebecca's cheeks as she sank into a nearby chair. "I…I simply don't know what to say."

"Say yes. Mrs. Johnson is a bully. Our marriage will silence her. I'll speak with the pastor today and—"

"No."

"—schedule the ceremony at once." His words came to a halt. "What did you say?"

"I said, no." She rose cautiously, her palms flat on her thighs as though to brace herself. "I won't marry you."

"You're turning me down? After everything that's happened today?"

"No. I mean, *yes.* I'm turning you down."

"Your reputation—"

"Is my concern, not yours."

She sniffed, rather loudly, but she didn't give in to her emotions. Oh, she blinked. And blinked. And *blinked.* But no tears spilled from her eyes.

Pete pulled in a hard breath. He'd never been more baffled by a woman. "We were both in my storm cellar," he reminded her through a painfully tight jaw. "That means we share the burden of the consequences equally."

Blink, blink, blink. "My decision is final."

"So is mine. We'll be married by the end of the day."

Her breathing quickened to short, hard pants. And then…*at last*…it happened. One lone tear slipped from her eye.

"Rebecca, please," he whispered, knowing his soft manner came too late.

"No." She wrapped her dignity around her like a coat of iron-clad armor. "We have nothing more to say to each other."

Just as another tear plopped onto the toe of her shoe, she turned and rushed out of the kitchen.

Stunned, Pete stared at the empty space she'd occupied. "That," he said to himself, "could have gone better."

* * * * *

*Will Pete be able to change Rebecca's mind
and salvage her reputation?
Find out in HEARTLAND WEDDING
available in February 2010
only from Love Inspired Historical.*

REQUEST YOUR FREE BOOKS!

2 FREE INSPIRATIONAL NOVELS
PLUS 2
FREE
MYSTERY GIFTS

Love Inspired

HISTORICAL
INSPIRATIONAL HISTORICAL ROMANCE

YES! Please send me 2 FREE Love Inspired® Historical novels and my 2 FREE mystery gifts (gifts are worth about $10). After receiving them, if I don't wish to receive any more books, I can return the shipping statement marked "cancel". If I don't cancel, I will receive 4 brand-new novels every other month and be billed just $4.24 per book in the U.S. or $4.74 per book in Canada. That's a saving of over 20% off the cover price. It's quite a bargain! Shipping and handling is just 50¢ per book in the U.S. and 75¢ per book in Canada.* I understand that accepting the 2 free books and gifts places me under no obligation to buy anything. I can always return a shipment and cancel at any time. Even if I never buy another book, the two free books and gifts are mine to keep forever.

102 IDN E4LC 302 IDN E4LN

Name	(PLEASE PRINT)
Address	Apt. #
City	State/Prov.	Zip/Postal Code

Signature (if under 18, a parent or guardian must sign)

Mail to Steeple Hill Reader Service:
IN U.S.A.: P.O. Box 1867, Buffalo, NY 14240-1867
IN CANADA: P.O. Box 609, Fort Erie, Ontario L2A 5X3
Not valid for current subscribers to Love Inspired Historical books.

Want to try two free books from another series?
Call 1-800-873-8635 or visit www.morefreebooks.com.

* Terms and prices subject to change without notice. Prices do not include applicable taxes. Sales tax applicable in N.Y. Canadian residents will be charged applicable provincial taxes and GST. Offer not valid in Quebec. This offer is limited to one order per household. All orders subject to approval. Credit or debit balances in a customer's account(s) may be offset by any other outstanding balance owed by or to the customer. Please allow 4 to 6 weeks for delivery. Offer available while quantities last.

Your Privacy: Steeple Hill Books is committed to protecting your privacy. Our Privacy Policy is available online at www.SteepleHill.com or upon request from the Reader Service. From time to time we make our lists of customers available to reputable third parties who may have a product or service of interest to you. If you would prefer we not share your name and address, please check here. ☐

Help us get it right—We strive for accurate, respectful and relevant communications. To clarify or modify your communication preferences, visit us at www.ReaderService.com/consumerschoice.

LIH10

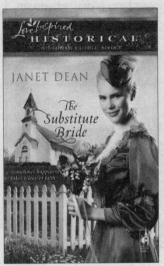

Love Inspired
HISTORICAL
INSPIRATIONAL HISTORICAL ROMANCE

Elizabeth Manning is desperate to avoid a forced marriage, so she exchanges places with a mail-order bride, praying widowed Iowa farmer Ted Logan will accept her as his new wife. Ted's gentleness and steadfast faith soon have Elizabeth yearning for the impossible—his love and a family for a lifetime.

Look for

The Substitute Bride

by

JANET DEAN